Books by Patrick Logan

Chase Adams FBI Thrillers

Book 1: Frozen Stiff

Book 2: Shadow Suspect

Book 3: Drawing Dead

Book 4: Amber Alert

Book 4.5: Georgina's Story

Book 5: Dirty Money

Book 6: Devil's Den

Book 7: Painted Ladies

Book 8: Adverse Effects

Dr. Beckett Campbell Medical Thrillers

Book 0: Bitter End

Book 1: Organ Donor

Book 2: Injecting Faith

Book 3: Surgical Precision

Book 4: Do Not Resuscitate

PRIZED FIGHT

Detective Damien Drake
Book 8

Patrick Logan

Don't quit. Suffer now and live the rest of your life as a champion.

–Muhammad Ali

Prologue

"**ARE YOU SURE YOU** don't want any meds? Not even a stiff drink? Because this *is* going to hurt."

Drake shook his head.

"No, I'm all right. I'm a big boy—I can take it."

The bespectacled man hovering over him just stared for a moment, clearly giving Drake time to change his mind. When Drake's only reply was to open wide, the man shrugged.

"All right, if you say so."

With that, he leaned forward and pressed the now whirring drill to the spot in Drake's gums that had once held a tooth.

The pain was instantaneous, and it was also tremendous. It ripped through Damien Drake's entire body like a bolt of lightning. He'd been through a lot in his thirty-eight years, but this was next level agony. He gripped the wooden armrests so tightly that he imagined crushing the wood, turning it into tinder. If the pain got any worse, this fantasy was likely to diffuse into reality.

When blood started to spill over his lower lip, the dentist retracted the drill, and Drake turned his head to the side. He didn't so much spit out the viscous fluid as it simply leaked from between his lips and splattered into the bucket that Kevin held to his chin.

Kevin, who had let him stay at the luxury resort in the Virgin Gorda in exchange for 'security duties', despite the fact that the place no longer required such services. They had a lot in common, Drake realized early on; the mild-mannered man from Nova Scotia had lost his cousin less than a year ago— who, strangely, was also named Kevin. He was a good influence on Drake, encouraging him to quit the booze and start taking care of his body. The transition from a functional alcoholic to something aseptic had been a difficult one, and the process hadn't been without setbacks. But with Kevin's help, he'd more or less succeeded. Most days, Drake spent much of his time talking to Kevin about everything from his nightmares—which had become more palatable after he'd stopped drinking—to how the Yankees had missed out by not signing Manny Machado or Mike Trout.

They weren't just friends; they were *good* friends.

But that had been then, and this was now.

The drill changed things.

I fucking hate you, Drake thought as he stared into the man's wide brown eyes. *I really,* really *hate you.*

"You ready for another go?" the dentist asked, moving the drill back toward his open mouth.

When Kevin had first come to Drake and mentioned the dentist who liked to frequent the Virgin Gorda—a man who never traveled anywhere without his dentistry kit—he'd jumped at the idea of calling in a favor.

After all, what better way to reinvent oneself than with a new, pearly white smile?

It appeared that despite all the changes he'd made, rash decisions such as this one was still part of his makeup.

"No," Drake said bluntly.

The dentist pulled back, a curious expression on his face. He started to say something, likely to ask Drake if he was sure he didn't want anything for the pain, but Kevin silenced him with an encouraging nod.

Yep, it's official; I hate you.

"Okay then," the dentist said before filling Drake's mouth with the drill.

He was pretty sure that he blacked out then, because the next thing Drake knew, his tongue was pressing up against the back of a brand-spanking new resin tooth that had been screwed into his jaw.

He gagged, spat, then managed to stutter a string of obscenities.

"The feeling's mutual," Kevin said with a laugh.

His head spinning, Drake sat up, thanked the dentist, and was dead set on punching Kevin in the face when a man suddenly appeared in the doorway of the makeshift operating room.

It was the unflappable maître d', a man who'd dealt with human traffickers, drug lords, and worse—all before Drake's arrival, of course. During his tenure, Drake had seen him placate difficult and often powerful guests, the most amusing of which included dealing with twelve entitled, trust fund douchebags who'd trashed a villa and were refusing to pay for damages.

It had taken just ten minutes of speaking to them before they'd apologized and paid in full—plus a fifteen percent tip, of course. But now, the man appeared agitated and uncomfortable. Kevin must have realized this too because he dropped the playful banter and quickly hurried over.

As they exchanged hushed words, the dentist took this opportunity to instruct Drake on the proper care of his new tooth.

Drake didn't hear a single word the man said.

Kevin turned to him, his tanned face suddenly going pale. "Drake?"

Alarm bells rang inside his head and he immediately peeled himself out of the chair.

"Yeah? What is it?"

"There's a… there's a call for you," Kevin said quietly.

Drake wasn't sure if he'd heard right. There couldn't be a call for him, because nobody knew he was here. The Virgin Gorda was part of the British Virgin Islands, which meant that they had an extradition treaty with the US. If someone from New York, someone in the NYPD, say, knew he was here, they could conceivably have him arrested for his outstanding warrants back in the US.

Kevin knew this, of course, and for the past six months either nobody had come looking for him, or the man had had his back.

Until now.

"What do you mean, there's a call for me?"

"I know, I know… we *both* know that your situation is complicated. But… it's a friend of yours, Drake." As he spoke, Kevin shot eyes at the dentist. Realizing that the temperature of the room had changed, the man held up his hands.

"My work here is done," he said as he quickly packed up his things. "Don't mind me."

As he waited for the dentist to leave the villa, Drake pushed his tongue in the space between his teeth, only to find it blocked by a foreign object.

This new tooth is going to take some getting used to.

Kevin hurried over to him, a cell phone on mute resting in the palm of his hand.

Drake had known that this time would come, that he couldn't run from his home forever. And New York City, for all its faults, for all its *many* faults, was indeed his home.

And yet, Drake didn't immediately grab the phone; instead, he just stared at it.

Don't answer it—you don't have to answer it. You don't owe anybody.

But Drake knew that if someone had reached him here after being off the grid for the better part of six months, then it must be serious. And when someone needed him, he simply couldn't stay away; that hadn't changed either.

He took a deep breath, grabbed the phone, and pressed it to his ear.

"Hello?"

"Drake?" a familiar voice replied. "I think... I think it's time you came back. We need your help."

PART I

Permanent Knockout

Chapter 1

"OH, I'M SORRY," THE woman with the dark hair said. She placed both palms on the lapels of the man's suit jacket and casually smoothed them.

He smiled down at her.

"Not a problem," he replied. The man's voice, like the rest of him, was full and bombastic, audible despite the dozens of people that milled about Grand Central Terminal.

The woman offered him a tired smile, then turned and quickly dissolved into the crowd, becoming just another nameless person desperate to get home and put their feet up after another busy workweek.

***

Dirt was smeared across the man's dark face and there was a half-empty bottle of Old English at his feet, even though he barely looked old enough to drink. His eyelids were at half-mast, and he was breathing deeply. If it weren't for the bustle of Grand Central Station, despite it being a Saturday, one might even be able to make out his soft snores. Clutched in a gloved hand—a glove with the fingers cut away—was an old

Starbucks cup with a ragged rim. The name on the side read, *Lizzy*. Instead of coffee within, however, there were a handful of coins and three curled up one-dollar bills.

A woman wearing a tan-colored Mac and a paisley scarf dropped a rolled-up bill into the cup as she passed. It struck the bottom with a dull '*thock*' and the man stirred.

"Thank you kindly," he grumbled, his eyes opening just wide enough to see her face. The woman didn't smile back. In fact, she didn't even acknowledge him. Instead, she just continued on her way.

When she was out of sight, the man rose to his feet and stretched his back, groaning as his spinal cord straightened. Cup in hand, he started in the opposite direction of the generous woman, but he only managed two steps before a hand came down on his shoulder. Heart racing now, the homeless man whipped around, moving his cup of money protectively to his chest as he did. But it wasn't a security guard or a member of the boys in blue who'd accosted him, but a handsome man with the beginnings of a beard and thick, dark hair.

"You forgot something."

At first, the homeless man wasn't sure what the newcomer was referring to. He clarified by leveling an outstretched finger at the bottle of Old English that was now lying on its side, lonely and abandoned.

"You can have it," the homeless man said, once again turning to leave. The hand on his shoulder, however, held fast.

"It's not my brand. Besides, it's a little early for me to start drinking."

The homeless man looked at the bottle, then turned his gaze to the man in the sports coat.

The latter finally let go and held his palms up.

"It's not my brand either," the homeless man snarled and then started to walk away.

"You shouldn't litter! It's not good to litter!" the man shouted after him, but his only response was to pick up the pace.

***

The woman peeled off her coat as she walked, then seamlessly tucked her scarf into an empty sleeve. She dropped both into a wire garbage can without even slowing. Beneath, she sported a dark suit that accentuated but fell just short of showing off her athletic physique. After a quick once over to make sure that none of the buttons on her white blouse had come undone beneath her coat, she made her way outside. Holding her hand high, she made her way through the throng of people waiting for a cab. She made sure that her movements were authoritative and not aggressive.

It worked; within moments, a taxi pulled up right in front of her and she got in.

"Where to, lady?" The driver asked, his beady eyes staring up at her in the rearview mirror. "I can take you as far west as Chelsea, but that's it. Gotta start shuttling people to MSG for the fight."

The woman removed her cell phone from her pocket and stared at the screen.

"Central Station," she said.

"Lady, you're at Central Station," the man replied.

The woman looked up and met the driver's eyes.

"Do a lap and bring me back here," she instructed.

The man opened his mouth, but she preemptively stymied his protests by handing over a fifty-dollar bill.

"Whatever you say," the man mumbled as he turned his eyes frontward and shifted the taxi into drive.

***

The homeless man's gait changed as he moved, transitioning from a stumble into something more adroit. He peeled off his soiled outerwear and jammed it into a drawstring backpack. Then he used the wet wipes hidden in the palms of his gloves to clear the dirt off his face. After dropping them in a garbage can, he smoothed the front of his *Nike* T-shirt and pulled a plastic lid from his pocket. It was a perfect fit, despite the ragged top of the Starbucks cup. Satisfied that none of his hard-earned cash would spill out, he broke into a jog.

After several sets of stairs, the man arrived on the platform just as the 6 was pulling into the station. He squeezed onto the subway train but didn't take a seat, even though several were available. Instead, he made his way to the opposite end of the train and then stood by the doors. When the subway stopped at 33rd street, he hopped off, then immediately boarded another train heading back to Grand Central.

This time, when the Brooklyn Bridge-bound 6 arrived, he got on the third to last train and took up residence beside a man with a shaved head and short goatee. A few seconds before the doors closed, a woman in a power suit pushed her way on and sat on the other side of the man.

None of them said a word until the fourth stop.

"Did you get it?" the man with the goatee asked, leaning to his right.

"Yeah, I got it," the young man replied with a grin. He removed the lid from his Starbucks cup and looked inside.

His smile immediately vanished.

Instead of seeing the ten-dollar bill with the elastic band wrapped around it within, all he saw were a handful of pennies. Even the three singles he'd had in there before the woman had dropped the tenner in were gone.

"Shit," he grumbled. "It was in there... I *had* it. Where the fuck did it go?"

Chapter 2

SCREECH THREW THE DOOR to SLH Investigations wide and burst through. The lights automatically came on, illuminating the three desks near the front.

"I don't understand how you could've lost it," he said through gritted teeth. "Everything else went according to plan. How the hell could you lose it?"

"I don't know," Leroy replied, his eyes downcast. "I don't know what the hell happened, man. I mean, I did everything like you said: as soon as Hanna dropped the tenner in, I stood, put the lid on, then got on the subway. Nobody talked to me and I never put the cup down. Shit, no one even came near me."

"Well, if you didn't lose it, maybe you, Hanna, didn't even put it in this cup."

Hanna crossed her arms over her chest and offered Screech an expression that made him immediately regret his choice of words.

"I took it from the DA and put it in his cup," she said flatly.

Screech shook his head and sat behind his desk. Then he leaned back in his chair and looked at the two other co-owners of SLH Investigations.

Co-owners…

The word had a strange ring to it and not just because Screech had started off as a simple tech analyst under Drake, but because soon there would be nothing to co-own.

They were bleeding out—had been for the last six months or so. All the money that Banksy had made him from Bitcoin had either been sunk into rent or lost in the market. Or stolen—he still wasn't sure what the shady money manager had done with their funds. All Screech knew was that they were broke.

But that was supposed to change—it *should've* changed. This job, as dangerous and shady as it was, would have kept them afloat for at least another three months. Screech also knew that success in this endeavor would have led to many other jobs. And his plan had been sound, solid.

But somewhere along the line, a link in their chain had been broken.

"Okay, okay," he said with a sigh. "Blame isn't going to help us. What we need to do is to go over what happened step-by-step, then from there we can try to figure out what went wrong."

"And more importantly, how to get the USB drive back," Hanna said. "Because I'm pretty sure that Mr. Petrazzino isn't going to be too happy about a fuck-up of this magnitude."

Yeah, no shit.

"Wasn't me, man. I did everything according to plan," Leroy said defensively.

Screech held up his hand.

"No blame, no blame. Let's just try to figure this out—Hanna, tell me exactly what happened."

Hanna appeared annoyed but eventually spoke up.

"I spotted the mark at Grand Central around six-thirty—the DA is a hard man to miss. As expected, he was moving quickly and there was some separation between him and his security detail. I bumped into him and lifted the USB drive from the inside pocket of his suit jacket. The man never suspected a thing. Then I wrapped it in a ten-dollar-bill, put an elastic around it, and dropped it into Leroy's cup. That's it, that's all—that's all she wrote."

"Did anybody follow you?"

Hanna shook her head.

"Nope. Even did the loop, though I don't think it was necessary. The man had no clue that he was robbed."

Screech nodded and turned to Leroy next.

"What about you?"

Leroy shrugged.

"I sat on the ground exactly where I was supposed to, playing a bum—by the way, we need to talk about these racial stereotypes. First, I'm a doorman with a ridiculous name, then I have to—"

"Damn it, Leroy, just tell me what happened. Please, it's late, I'm tired, and we just need to find the USB."

"Fine, fine. Look, I sat there until Hanna dropped the USB key in my cup and then got up." Leroy paused for a second, which did not go unnoticed by either Screech or Hanna. "Then I put the lid on the cup and—"

"No, go back. Did anything happen *after* Hanna put the USB drive in your cup before you put the lid on."

Leroy's eyes drifted up and to the left as he struggled to recall the exact sequence of events.

"Yeah," he said hesitantly, "but I don't think it meant anything."

"You don't think *what* meant anything?" Hanna snapped.

"Well, something weird did happen. I was just starting to walk away from my spot on the ground when this guy told me to go pick up my bottle of Old English. I told him I didn't want it and he said something about not littering. I told you it didn't mean anything."

Hanna raised an eyebrow.

"You had a bottle of OE with you?"

"Just conforming to stereotypes, playing the role."

Sensing that they were veering off course again, Screech piped up.

"What did this guy look like? Was he part of the DA's security detail?"

"I don't think so—white guy, medium build. Brown hair, a bit of a beard. Good-looking, I guess."

Screech chewed his lip for a second.

"Did this guy ever touch you? Did he—"

There was a sudden knock on the door that was so jarring that Screech leaned back in his chair and then was launched forward again.

"Fuck," he grumbled. "Who the hell is coming at this hour?"

His eyes drifted to the dark shadow behind the frosted glass. Something didn't feel right about the situation, and it wasn't just the time, either. It was also the veracity of the knock and the entire situation—including the powerful nature of both parties involved in the now botched job—that put Screech on edge. But before he could say anything to this effect, Leroy was already at the door and reaching for the handle.

"Maybe someone found the USB key," he said with a shrug.

Screech leaped from his chair.

"Leroy, wait!"

But he was too late. The second that the lock was disengaged, the door was shoved open so hard that it bashed into Leroy's face and sent him staggering backward.

Chapter 3

"I KNEW I'D FIND you here!" the man who barged into SLH Investigations shouted. His finger was pointed directly at Hanna, who looked as if she'd seen a ghost.

"What the fuck?" Screech barked as he moved between the man and Hanna. He cast a glance over his shoulder to Leroy, who was holding his nose and moaning. Blood leaked from between his fingers, but his injury didn't appear serious. "Who the hell—"

"Hanna, come over here!"

The man had a shaved head and close-set eyes that were red with anger.

"Hold up, hold up!" Hanna exclaimed, moving backward.

"I don't know who you are but if you don't get out of here right now—"

"You don't even know who I am?" The man seemed surprised by this and cocked his head to one side. "Seriously?"

As he spoke, the man took two large strides forward, and now it was Screech who was backing up.

"No, I have no idea—"

"Hanna? We were married for six years and your partners don't even know who I am? Seriously? Did our time together mean nothing? *Nothing?*"

Married? What the hell?

Screech wasn't sure what was more surprising, the fact that Hanna had been married or that she had been married to *this* man. He looked to Leroy once more, hoping that he'd collected himself and would be able to offer some support, but he was still moaning and clutching his face.

Screech swallowed hard. Hanna's ex-husband, if that's who he really was, had at least three inches and sixty pounds on him. Maybe more, depending on how much bulk he carried beneath his thick overcoat.

"Jimmy, you need to leave. You need to get out of here before I call the cops," Hanna warned. The slight tremor in her voice amped up Screech's anxiety. For as long as he'd known the woman, Screech had only seen her frightened once: when she'd been trapped in the basement of the Loomis Estate and had nearly been murdered.

"The only way I'm leaving here is with you by my side," Jimmy growled.

Screech couldn't believe what was happening. The day had gone from terrible to absolutely brutal. And it was starting to escalate even further.

"Listen, I'm sure—"

Screech didn't see the shove, but he certainly felt it. For a big man, this Jimmy, Hanna's ex-husband, was lightning-quick. His left hand shot out and struck Screech in the left shoulder, sending him flying backward. He collided with his desk, toppling it. His computer monitor crashed to the floor and the desk drawer flung open, sending its contents scattering across the tiles like plastic vomit.

And that's what Screech felt like doing as he lay curled up into a ball, trying to, at the very least, make it onto all fours: vomiting.

His diaphragm was paralyzed, his gut hurt, and his head was spinning.

Still, he was cognizant enough to recognize that even though he wasn't seriously injured, it was only a matter of time before he was.

Jimmy lumbered over to him, but he lost his footing on a stray pen and dropped to a knee.

This might have saved Screech, or maybe it just prolonged the inevitable.

"Hey big fella, you should think long and hard about what you're going to do next. The cops are on their way," a voice that Screech didn't recognize shouted from behind them.

At long last, Screech managed to get onto his knees and turn. The strange voice belonged to Leroy who was standing in the doorway, his cell phone pressed to his ear.

Jimmy chuckled.

"You didn't call the cops."

Screech didn't know if his partner had called the cops, but given SLH Investigations' reputation, even if he had, there was no guarantee that they would actually show up.

"Maybe I did, maybe I didn't," Leroy replied. Then he turned his head to one side and spat blood on the floor.

I don't know what game you're playing, Leroy, but I would stick to 'maybe we did' if we want to get out of this in one piece.

"I'm guessing you didn't. And I'm also guessing—"

Leroy suddenly brought the hand not holding the phone out in front of him.

"Like I said, maybe I did, maybe I didn't," he repeated, this time with a smirk on his face.

For a man who'd only held a gun once before in his life, Leroy looked pretty comfortable with it. At least he had the business end aimed in the right direction.

Jimmy froze, which gave Screech the time he needed to rise to his feet.

"That's it, that's a good boy," Leroy said, gesturing towards the door with the barrel of the gun. "Why don't you see yourself out."

Okay, fantastic idea; enrage this furious bull.

Jimmy did as he was instructed but was determined to have the last word. As he stepped through the door, he turned back and once again pointed his finger at Hanna's chest.

"This isn't over, Hanna. I'm gonna come back for you. I'm going to come back for you real soon."

Chapter 4

"**GIVE ME THAT BEFORE** you shoot your dick off," Hanna snapped, grabbing the gun out of Leroy's hand. Leroy didn't resist; in fact, he looked relieved.

"What in the holy hell was that about?" Screech demanded. His side was sore from where it had struck his desk, but he wasn't really hurt.

His desk and its contents, on the other hand, had taken a beating.

"I'm sorry," Hanna replied, returning the gun to her desk and lowering her gaze. "I didn't think he'd ever find me."

Screech stared at her for a moment before shaking his head and facing Leroy.

"Did you really call the cops?"

Leroy, who was dabbing his nose with a tissue, showed Screech his cell phone.

"Battery's dead."

Screech made a face.

"You don't think, do you, Leroy?"

Leroy pulled the bloody Kleenex from his face and glared at him.

"What the hell was I supposed to do? Hanna's psycho boyfriend was going to kick your ass, maybe even kill you. I had no other choice."

Screech ground his teeth in frustration.

"No other choice? Really? What if he came at you... were you going to shoot him?"

"You should be thanking Leroy, not chastising him, Screech."

Screech whipped around.

"Really? I made a promise to the boy's mother that he wouldn't be in any dangerous situations. I'm not going back on that promise, and I'm not going to be the one responsible for any of your bad decisions."

"That's your problem, Screech," Hanna shot back. "We're in this thing together—you're not our almighty ruler, you don't have to take responsibility for what we do. Shit, you said we were partners in this thing, but all you've done since Drake left is to try to control everything. So, what did you want Leroy to do? Huh? Grab another phone and call the cops for real? That's a fantastic idea... hopefully your buddy Sergeant Yasiv shows up and asks more questions about Captain Loomis and what—"

"Enough!" Screech suddenly roared. Not an angry man in general, ever since Drake had gone missing, these sorts of outbursts had become more commonplace. It dawned on him that this overbearing sense of responsibility was probably the reason why Drake came off as an asshole most of the time. Still, this realization did little to calm his anger at that moment. "Sure, we're in this together... until you guys fuck up again. You lost the goddamn USB key, which was the only way that we could keep our doors open for another day. And let's not forget that it was your husband that broke in here and fucked up my desk and broke Leroy's nose."

"I don't think it's broken," Leroy remarked.

Screech was seeing red now, but it was Hanna who had more to say.

"All, so *we're* to blame, is that it? What the hell were you doing when we were trying to steal from the goddamn district attorney of all people—which is a contract that you, and you alone, accepted, in case you forgot. The way I see it? Leroy and I took all the risk while you were beating your meat on the subway."

Screech looked skyward.

"I made the plan, remember? It was *my* plan, and things would've worked out perfectly if you guys just did what you were supposed to."

"Oh, that's your job, is it? That's your role? The mastermind? And what, pray tell, are your qualifications, if you don't mind me asking? It can't possibly be past success, that's for sure. The last time you came up with a master plan, Leroy almost got beat up, I almost got killed, and you ended up shooting—"

"That's it," Screech said as he made his way toward the door near the back of the office. It was labeled as a broom closet, but it was actually a private consultation area that was reserved for discussions that couldn't take place out in the open. Not that they had much use for it lately, but the entire office seemed superfluous at this point. "That's it."

"Where are you going?" Leroy asked after blowing his nose. "Screech?"

"He's running away," Hanna replied for him.

"I'm not running away—I'm getting a drink."

With that, he strode past a glaring Hanna and pulled the door to the consultation room wide. As he rummaged through his desk in search of what little was left of the Johnny Blue reserved for Drake, he heard Hanna grumble something about how helpful booze had been for their once eponymous leader—the D in DSLH Investigations, the D that had long since been scratched off.

Screech held the bottle in one hand and stared at the man with the cane and the top hat on the label. Then he slammed the door closed and removed the cork.

Chapter 5

AFTER TEN OR MAYBE fifteen minutes in his own head, and a couple fingers of scotch deep, Screech's fury dissipated. He knew that if they had any chance of keeping SLH Investigations open, they were going to have to band together. He felt oddly like one half of a dysfunctional marriage, despite the fact that he hadn't had a real relationship since his late teens. And, as was the case with most marriages destined for divorce, the real cause of their recent argument centered around finances.

Speaking of divorce, how the hell did Hanna neglect to mention that she'd been married before? Especially given the fact that her ex-husband is a bona fide psychopath?

He shook his head and picked up three glasses.

When he opened the broom closet door, he was surprised to see that someone had righted his desk and had put his things back in the drawer. His monitor had a large crack going from corner to corner, which would be expensive to replace, but right now, two computers were more than enough to handle zero clients. Hanna was sitting behind her desk, looking at him with something akin to pity on her face.

And Leroy… well, Leroy with a 'not broken' nose, was just staring off into space.

"You done with your little hissy fit?" Hanna asked. She may pity him, but Hanna was still Hanna.

"I come bearing gifts—a truce," Screech proclaimed, holding up the three glasses. He plopped them onto her desk and poured Johnnie Blue into two of them. After shoving one in Hanna's direction, he grabbed the other.

"What about me?" Leroy asked as he made his way toward them.

Screech looked down at the empty glass and shrugged.

"I thought OE was more your style?"

"Very funny," Leroy grumbled.

They sipped their drinks in silence for a few moments, before Screech addressed the elephant in the room.

"I didn't know you're married."

"I'm not," Hanna corrected.

"Fair enough—*were* married. What the hell was that all about?"

"That was about Jimmy being Jimmy."

Screech sighed and took a drink. This was like pulling teeth.

"Care to talk about it?"

"Nope."

"Look, I don't mean to pry into your personal life, but when someone barges through the door and threatens all of us, I think we have a right to know a little bit more than you're giving us."

Hanna looked at her glass and then finally relented.

"That was my ex-husband Jimmy—we were married for about six years, then we got divorced." She paused for a moment, hoping that this was enough. The expression on Screech's face indicated otherwise. "What else do you want to know? We got divorced because he's just too lovable. You know, he was just too much of a nice guy, too doting. I'm surprised you didn't pick up on that earlier."

"Yeah, sure. But what are we gonna do about him?"

"We're not going to do anything about him. He's an asshole. I've already got a restraining order against him, and he's on parole. He knows better than to fuck with me."

Screech scoffed.

"Well, maybe he just forgot then. Or maybe *you* forgot that he was just here and busted Leroy's—"

"It's not broken."

"—nose and almost knocked me into next week. If he's on parole, we should call his PO."

Hanna shook her head.

"I'll deal with it."

"How? Because I mean—"

"Screech, I said I'll deal with it."

Feeling another fight coming on, Screech let it go—for now, anyway. He didn't want a recurrence at the office, nor did he want anything to happen to her. Hanna was as tough as they came, but she was still human.

Probably.

"Okay, okay. So, let's get back to what happened this afternoon. Leroy, the man who told you not to litter… was he one of DA Trumbo's goons? A member of his security detail?"

"I don't think so," Leroy replied. "I didn't recognize him from the pictures we reviewed before heading to Grand Central Station."

Screech shook his head. He'd thought that things would get easier once Mayor Ken Smith fled New York. But the vacancy had only made people feral in the never-ending pursuit of power.

There was intense pressure for potential suitors for Mayor to have squeaky clean records or, rather, to make sure that their skeletons remained not in closets but buried at the bottom of the ocean.

And pressure made people do things that they normally wouldn't dream of.

Case in point, Screech and SLH Investigations.

Screech had known who Nick Petrazzino was before the man came into his office, of course. But even if he hadn't, the fact that he wanted Screech to steal from the acting District Attorney of New York County, Mark Trumbo, was a pretty big hint. Sure, Nick said all the right things, claiming that the USB key actually belonged to him and had been stolen and that the DA was a bad man who, should he be elected mayor, would be even worse than Ken Smith. Screech had used these talking points to rationalize the decision to accept the contract, even though he knew that getting involved with Nick and his crew would eventually come back to haunt them.

The truth was, they were desperate.

And, despite what Hanna said, their plan had been a good one—it had been nearly perfect.

Screech had learned early on under Drake's tutelage that people were accustomed or even beholden to their routines. Even when they tried to mix things up, these deviations became fairly predictable. Which was why when they'd gotten wind of the DA heading to Grand Central Station on Saturday evening before a big boxing match at MSG, they were all set. And given Hanna's surprising pickpocket skills and Leroy's Oscar-winning acting, it should've been a slam-dunk.

Except it wasn't.

"Hanna, can you pull up the pictures of the DA's security detail to see if Leroy recognizes any of them. Just in case."

"Sure," she said, clearly grateful for the change of subject.

As Screech settled in behind her chair, Leroy spoke up.

"Even if it was one of them, that just raises a bigger question."

"Yeah? And what question is that?" Screech asked.

"Why in the hell would they steal the USB back? Why didn't they just arrest me on the spot?"

"No idea," Screech said as Hanna pulled up photographs of the DA's security detail.

"No, it's definitely none of those Bobos," Leroy confirmed.

"You sure?"

"I'm sure."

"So, if you didn't drop it, and the DA's security didn't take it, what the hell happened to it?" Screech asked.

Leroy shrugged.

"Maybe someone else targeted us and stole it," he offered.

Screech pinched the bridge of his nose. Things were unduly complicated as it was without introducing another party into the equation.

"Like who? Who would —"

There was another loud bang on the door and Screech immediately fell silent.

Chapter 6

"DON'T EVEN THINK ABOUT it, Leroy," Screech warned as he backed away from Hanna's desk and made his way toward his own. Once again, he spied a dark figure through the frosted glass. Intended to offer them some privacy from the outside world, Screech was quickly beginning to regret not opting for a regular pane.

Why didn't you put up a security camera, you dork? You set up half a dozen in Mrs. Armatridge's place, but didn't think about protecting your own office?

The knock came again and as Screech reached beneath his desk, he offered a menacing stare at Leroy. It was unnecessary, however; neither he nor Hanna had moved.

Confident that they would stay put until further instruction, Screech felt around for the holster taped to the underside of his desk. His searching fingers found the worn leather and he grabbed the butt of the gun and pulled it out.

Or, at least, that's what he *tried* to do. The problem was, his hand came back empty.

"What the hell?"

Confused, Screech dropped his head down and stared at the holster. It was there attached with duct tape just as he'd left it, but it was empty.

He straightened and turned to Hanna and Leroy.

"You guys seen my gun? When you were cleaning up my desk, did you see my gun?" he asked, trying not to sound desperate.

It wasn't just the fact that if Jimmy had returned, he needed a weapon of some sort, it was also the importance of this gun in particular. Or, rather, what he'd done with said gun.

Leroy shrugged.

"I didn't see it."

"Me neither," Hanna concurred.

"I put it back in the holster," he whispered. "I know I did."

Screech quickly replayed what had happened at the Loomis Estate in his mind. He remembered getting out of the car and telling Leroy to stay put. With sirens filling the night air, patrons were fleeing out the front doors and desperately trying to get their keys from a fear-stricken valet.

He'd gone against the crowd, heading toward the back of the Estate. Screech had hoped to find Hanna, but he'd come across Jasmine instead. And that's when he saw Captain Brandon Loomis. The man, larger than life, bombastically bragged about how he was going to bring ANGUIS Holdings back, with or without Ken Smith.

How he was going to restart the nightmare that had gripped New York City for years over again.

Until the point when the gun went off, Screech hadn't even realized it was in his hand. In the chaos, the only person who had witnessed what he'd done was Jasmine and she was long gone.

But as he'd turned and hurried back to his car, Screech could have sworn he'd seen two other people in the distance, one with a handkerchief shoved in her mouth and another — a man he didn't recognize, a man with —

"Screech?" Hanna said, her face riddled with concern.

He shook his head.

"My gun — you sure you haven't seen it?"

It had been his intention of getting rid of the damn thing, of course, but he'd been worried that someone would find it and be able to trace it back to him. And then he'd just simply forgotten about it, up until Sergeant Yasiv's recent visit, of course.

The heavy knocking came again, and Screech uttered a curse under his breath.

"Here, use mine," Hanna offered, holding her pistol out to him. Screech made a face but nodded and reached for it.

The second the butt touched his palm, Screech's heart started to race again. He gripped it tightly and turned it over in his palm, trying not to visualize shooting Captain Loomis.

A shudder coursed through him, and Screech nearly dropped the gun.

"Screech? You okay?" Leroy asked.

Screech clenched his teeth and regained his focus.

"Fine," he said out of the corner of his mouth. And then, as he made his way toward the door, he sucked in a deep breath and tried to make his voice sound as intimidating as possible.

"Jimmy, you need to think long and hard about you're doing. We're armed in here, and if you don't leave now, you're going to regret it."

The figure on the other side of the glass stopped fidgeting, and Screech waited for what he thought would come next: the rattling of the door handle, maybe a kick to the frame.

Sweat broke out on his brow. He would protect SLH, just as he'd protected Hanna and Jasmine at the Loomis Estate. He would do anything to ensure they were safe.

But the figure made no attempt to enter.

"It's not... it's not Jimmy," an unfamiliar voice said.

Screech, thinking that this was a trick, moved to one side and then slowly approached the door.

"Who is it then?" he asked, keeping the gun trained on the dark shadow.

"My name's Brock... my name is Brock Page and I really need your help. Please... please open the door. I don't have much time."

Chapter 7

THE DARK-SKINNED MAN'S face was so badly bruised that it took several moments before Screech noticed the gun in his hands. He had a cut on his lip, a lump on his temple, and his left eye was so swollen that it was barely open.

"Who the hell are—"

And then Screech saw the gun. Brock was holding it in both outstretched palms like some sort of burnt offering.

Screech immediately raised his own pistol and took a step back.

"Put it down... put the gun down!"

"Take it," the man said. As if to emphasize his point, he extended his arms.

But after what had happened with Jimmy, Screech was taking no chances.

"I said, put it down!"

Despite the clear instructions, Brock seemed at a loss for what to do. In his periphery, Screech saw Leroy stride forward.

"Leroy, get back."

But like the bruised man, Leroy also seemed to have a hard time following instructions; his hand darted out like a Cobra's strike and grabbed the gun.

"What? He said he didn't want it," Leroy explained with a shrug.

Hanna, her own hand wrapped in a tissue, retrieved the gun from Leroy. Brock evidently misinterpreted this as an invitation to enter SLH, as he stepped forward.

"No, no, no," Screech said, keeping the pistol trained on the man. "Back up—back the fuck up."

The man did as he was asked, his shoulders slumped.

"I need your help."

"And what I need, is for you to get the fuck out of here."

The man opened his mouth as if to say something further but decided against it. He bowed his head and started to turn back to the hallway.

Screech kept the gun trained on him the entire time.

"Brock," Leroy mumbled. "Brock Page... Brock Page... Brock Page..."

Screech gave an angry look. Leroy was chewing his lower lip, and one eye was squinted shut.

"What the hell is wrong with you?"

Leroy suddenly snapped his fingers and pointed at the man who was at least ten strides from the door now.

"Wait—did you say, Brock *Page*?"

The man's footsteps faltered, and Screech found himself shaking his head.

"Keep on walking—don't even think about turning around."

"Screech," Leroy implored in his ear. "That's Brock Page."

"Yeah, you only said that ten times."

"No, I think that's *Brock Page*, the boxer. WBA and WBC Super Middleweight champion."

"I don't care who he is."

"You sure?" Hanna piped up.

"Yeah, sure. That's him," Leroy replied.

Screech was getting annoyed now.

"Would you guys just—"

"Wait!" Hanna suddenly blurted. "Hey, Brock, wait a sec!"

What the hell is it now?

Screech resisted the urge to turn, and thankfully, Brock did as well.

"Wait!"

Hanna's voice was bordering on a shout now, and this time both Screech and Brock whipped around to face her.

"Hanna, what do you think you're—"

"Put the damn gun down, Screech," Hanna instructed, placing her hand on top of the barrel and forcing it to waist height.

Screech's annoyance had transitioned into confusion.

"Hanna? What's going on?"

She didn't answer him; instead, she gestured for Brock to come back. When the man's eyes darted to Screech and his now lowered pistol, Hanna shook her head.

"Come back."

With his eyes locked on Screech, Brock slowly made his way back toward SLH Investigations.

It took all of Screech's willpower not to raise the gun again and demand this man vacate the premises immediately. But his mind kept coming back to what Hanna had said earlier, about how this was their gig, how they had to make decisions together.

That he wasn't responsible for *their* actions.

I'll hear her out, Screech conceded after much deliberation. *I owe her that much. But I'm not letting go of this gun.*

He leveled his eyes at Hanna.

"Pow wow, *now*," he ordered. And then to Brock, Screech added, "You, step inside. Step inside and close the door. But if you so much as make a move after that? Don't think I won't use this."

Chapter 8

"THIS IS WHAT WE want," Hanna whispered. "What we *need*."

Screech looked over his shoulder at the man standing against the door, his bruised hands clasped in front of him. Hanna had wanted to go talk in the broom closet, but there was no way that Screech was letting this stranger out of his sight.

Not for a moment.

"What do you mean, this is what we want?" he asked, struggling to keep his voice down.

"Leroy, how much do you think that Brock Page is worth? I mean, I don't know that much about boxing, but…"

Leroy pushed his tongue into his cheek and looked skyward for a moment.

"I'd say fifteen? Twenty, maybe?"

"Fifteen what?" Screech demanded.

"Million," Hanna answered for him.

Screech's eyes went wide, and he once again looked over at Brock. He was badly bruised, battered, and desperate.

And… guilty? For some reason, he was giving off a guilty vibe.

"You're telling me that this guy is worth fifteen million dollars?"

Leroy shrugged.

"I'd say at least that. I mean, boxing isn't the draw that it was even ten years ago, but these guys still make bank."

Maybe it was the fact that Screech was still reeling from the clusterfuck that had been today, but he still wasn't following his partners' logic.

"This guy comes in here looking like he just got hit by a car and with a gun in his hands, and you're telling me this is what we want? That this is what SLH needs?"

"Well, no, not exactly," Hanna began, clearly annoyed now. "What we need is an infusion of cash. And that's what this man represents."

Screech was beginning to clue into the big picture now, but he trusted Brock Page just about as much as he trusted Hanna's psychotic ex-husband. And yet, he could already sense that this new SLH democracy was going to render him a hanging chad and that his vote simply wouldn't count.

"Why is it that everyone who comes to our door is all messed up?" he grumbled. "Why can't we just have normal clients for once?"

Leroy and Hanna exchanged a look.

"Because we're a PI firm, Screech," Hanna reminded him in a patronizing tone. "Who do you think needs a private investigator? Either women who think their husbands are cheating on them, or people like Brock Page over there who are in trouble and can't go to the cops. Haven't you read a single Raymond Chandler book?"

Before Screech could answer, Hanna turned to Leroy.

"Let's put this to a vote. Me? I want to hear him out. If his problem is something that we can take on, something that we can *bill* for, for once, I say we go for it. How about you, Leroy?"

Leroy immediately raised his hand and Screech rolled his eyes. He couldn't tell if the man was just enamored by the thought of working for a celebrity or if he was actually making a business-oriented decision.

And this is why uninformed people shouldn't be allowed to vote…

"That settles it then," Hanna said, not even looking to Screech for a vote.

If Drake were here... Screech thought, shaking his head, *if Drake were here, he'd have my back.*

"Fine, but if this gets shady, if I sense any danger, any at all, we aren't voting on whether or not I use this damn gun."

Not waiting for a reply, Screech immediately raised his eyes to Brock.

"You've got five minutes—five minutes to tell us what your problem is and then you're either going to jail or we're taking your case. So, now, why don't you illuminate us as to why, exactly, you showed up here all beat up holding a gun?"

Chapter 9

"I THINK... I THINK it's better if I show, rather than tell you," Brock Page suggested, his arms and hands still folded in front of him.

Screech immediately shook his head.

"No, I've seen this sort of thing before; you go on our computer, punch a few keys, install a rootkit and the next thing I know the FBI comes a-knockin' and arrests me for some kiddie porn ring."

Hanna groaned, but Screech wasn't done yet.

"Tell us—tell us why you came here looking the way you do with a gun in your hands."

"Look, I get it. I may have taken a knock or two to the head in my time," Brock pointed at the golf ball-sized lump on his temple, "but I'm not stupid. I just... I don't have much time. If you don't want me to use your computer, fine, just go on and look up my last fight. Shouldn't be hard, given the fact that it ended, oh, an hour and a half ago?"

"You fought tonight?" Screech asked, his jaw dropping.

Brock nodded, guilt once again spreading across his features.

"Yeah, yeah, I did." He paused for a moment, his gaze lowering to the floor. "Just watch the video. Please."

Screech looked over at Leroy, who had already taken up residence behind his desk and was busy searching the Internet. He moved behind him, as did Hanna, but when Brock started to do the same, Screech shook his head.

"Stay there," he instructed.

Brock nodded and did as he was asked.

For a WB-something or other boxing champion, he's damn polite, Screech thought. *Almost too polite.*

"All right," Leroy said, indicating his monitor. "I think I found it. You were fighting Shane Nolasco, right?"

"Yeah," Brock confirmed, his voice cracking.

Screech shook his head. He'd told Hanna and Leroy in no uncertain terms that the man was untrustworthy, but the truth was, Brock Page was almost impossible to figure out.

He was polite, demure, guilt-stricken, and obviously dangerous.

"Well, here it is… all one minute and forty seconds of it."

Screech reluctantly lowered his eyes with the intention of glancing up again a second later. But when he noticed the title of the video, he found it nearly impossible to look away: *WBA and WBC Champ Brock Page kills IBF pro Shane Nolasco in the Ring—MUST SEE BEFORE IT'S TAKEN DOWN.*

His throat suddenly dry, Screech tapped Leroy on the back and the man pressed play.

The video was much longer than two minutes, but Leroy skipped over all the lead-up, including the walk to the ring and the introductions, and went straight to the action. According to the voice of the commentator, the match started off just as everyone expected it would: a feeling out process, with the fighters throwing mainly weak jabs that missed their mark in order to find their range.

But then, around the one-minute mark, something changed.

Brock landed a stiff jab that, while partially blocked by Shane's forearm, sent him reeling. It didn't seem like a particularly violent blow to Screech, nor to the commentator who said something to that effect. But Shane never really regained his bearings after this initial blow.

Instead, he seemed disoriented and after another series of rather pedestrian jabs, Shane's hands started to drop. A straight right down the pipe sent the man's head flying backward, and the left hook that followed buckled his knees. He was already on the way down when Brock lunged with an uppercut that sent him sprawling to the canvas.

"Jesus," Leroy whispered. Screech shared the man's sentiment. After only a four-count, the ref immediately called the fight and then signaled for the doctors to enter the ring. As they tried to rouse him, Shane's legs started to quiver and shake. The camera then panned out, revealing the shocked faces of the twenty-thousand plus fans in attendance at Madison Square Garden.

"He died?" Leroy gasped as the video continued to play.

Screech looked at Brock and saw that his eyes were clenched shut. Even so, tears had wet the man's cheeks.

Who is this guy?

"That's what they said," Brock replied in a barely audible whisper. "That's what they said..."

Screech was still trying to wrap his mind around what had happened in the fight.

He knew that in boxing or any combat sport—any sport, really—there was a possibility of severe injury, and maybe even death. It was rare, certainly, but it was possible.

And yet, something about what Screech had just witnessed on screen didn't seem right, didn't seem at all natural.

Perhaps sensing his thoughts, or maybe just elucidating his own, Brock spoke up.

"He passed his physical. I mean, Shane was concussed about six months ago, but it was only a minor concussion and he'd fully recovered—he was fine. No slurred speech, no double vision, everything was good. Shit, we both had great camps, with no major injuries."

"Who told you this?" Screech asked, eyebrows raised. "The commission?"

Brock shook his head.

"No, the commission didn't tell me; Shane did."

This was getting more confusing by the second.

"Wait, *Shane* told you this? How do you know that your opponent wasn't lying? Maybe he had some underlying condition that he just didn't want to tell you or the commission."

Brock shuddered.

"Because Shane wasn't just my opponent… he was my friend. My *best* friend."

Chapter 10

SCREECH ACCEPTED THE CUP of coffee from Hanna and then watched as she poured one for Brock and then one for herself. Leroy abstained, claiming that caffeine made him jittery.

Hanna went as far as to offer Brock something stronger, against Screech's better judgment, but the man claimed not to drink.

Brock Page, it appeared, was full of surprises.

"Okay, okay, we need to know exactly what happened. I want to know about the lead-up to the fight, and then what happened afterward. Because so far as I could see in the video, Shane died from a fist and not a gun."

Brock nodded and started to open his mouth, but Screech wasn't done yet.

"But before you say anything else, we need to enlist you as a client. That way, anything you tell us will be confidential. This also comes at a cost. We're going to need a retainer and a *per diem*. And let me tell you, it ain't going to be cheap."

Brock nodded.

"How much?"

Screech looked over at Hanna for some support, but she just shrugged.

"For starters, there will be a twenty-five-thousand-dollar non-refundable retainer—we bill at two-fifty an hour."

Brock never stopped nodding.

"No problem."

"And," Screech continued, "you'll be picking up the tab for any video or audio surveillance equipment we need."

"Done."

"If anything else should—"

Brock spread his hands out on the table and leaned forward, raising his swollen eyes to meet Screech's.

"I'll pay whatever you want," he said bluntly. "If you find out what happened to my friend and what happened to my manager, I'll pay you whatever you want."

"Good. Now that we have that out of the way, what—wait, your manager? What happened to your manager?"

Brock was crestfallen.

"He's dead."

And that's where the gun comes in, Screech thought. *This just keeps getting better.*

"What happened?" Leroy asked.

"Wait, let's start at the beginning—tell us about Shane, tell us about how you know him."

Brock remained silent for some time, clearly trying to collect his thoughts and keep his emotions in check. When he spoke again, his voice was oddly flat.

"We grew up together. Back when we were kids, we both attended Pike's Boxing Gym—a shitty local joint that let us box for free if we helped clean up, that sort of thing. Owner was a guy named Carl Severson, still is. He's one of those guys who likes to keep the kids off the street. And in Tremont, if you're on the streets, you're likely slinging dope."

"I grew up in Tremont," Leroy said.

"Then you know what I'm talking about. Anyways, both me and Shane got pretty good in the ring, but I was the one who got picked up by a local promoter first. After my first paid gig, I left Pike's. My career kinda took off after that, while Shane's took a little while longer to get goin'. He left Pike's a year or so after I did. We both go back every once in a while, especially when we have fights here in New York. We kept in touch over the years, too, but you know how it is, life sometimes gets in the way."

As does money...

Even with limited information, Screech was already formulating a narrative in his mind; Shane was the lesser known of the two fighters and likely harbored some resentment toward his old friend.

And yet he was the one who'd ended up dead.

"What about this fight? Did you talk much before? You mentioned that Shane said he had a good camp..."

"When my manager Mark told me that he was working on a fight with Shane, I reached out to him. We both agreed that it was a good idea, especially because we both knew that we don't have too many fights left in us."

Brock suddenly paused, clearly not realizing what he was saying until it was too late. While the man collected himself, Screech reached for his coffee.

A quick glance at the clock showed that it was coming up to one thirty in the morning and with everything that had happened today—the botched robbery of the district attorney, followed by almost being murdered by Hanna's ex-husband, and now this—exhaustion was beginning to set in.

"I knew that Shane had a concussion in his last fight, so I asked him about it. He said he was fine, that he'd already been cleared by the commission to fight."

"Maybe he lied," Hanna suggested. "Maybe he hadn't fully recovered yet."

Brock looked at her.

"It wouldn't be the first time that a boxer lied about his injuries, cheated the tests to get cleared to fight. But the thing is, I saw him—I saw him spar, I saw him reading the paper, I even saw him with his—" Brock's voice hitched, "—with his daughter. He was *fine*. There's no way that a couple of jabs and an uppercut should've... should've..."

"Take your time," Hanna suggested.

"That's the thing... I don't *have* time. They're coming for me."

"What? Who's coming for you?" Leroy asked.

"The cops."

"The cops? Shane died in the ring and even though—"

Brock shook his head.

"No, not because of Shane... but because of my manager, Mark Magnusson."

Screech was dreading this part and wished that Hanna had offered him something stronger than coffee instead of Brock.

"What happened after the fight, Brock?" Screech asked.

The man rubbed the lump on the side of his head.

"After the fight, I went to Mark's house. And that's when I found him lying on the ground, a bullet in his head. A bullet from the very gun that you took from me as soon as I walked in here."

Chapter 11

"I WAS SCARED, MAN... I just killed my friend in the ring and I was fuckin' scared... so I ran. I mean, I even skipped out on the post-fight piss test, so I dunno if I'm even gonna get paid," Brock admitted. "Not that it matters now."

"Where were you going?" Screech asked, trying to keep the man on track.

"At first, I looked for Mark, but I couldn't find him anywhere. There were just so many people around, such chaos, that I just wanted to get out. I *had* to get out of there."

"Right, but *where* were you going?" Screech asked again.

Brock lowered his gaze.

"The first thing I thought of was Shane's wife and kid. I was going to her place, to tell her what happened when I got a text from Mark. It was all fuckin' cryptic... *I know what happened*, or some shit. I tried calling him, but it went straight to voicemail. So, I drove out to his place."

He paused, clearly uncomfortable with what followed. But Screech needed to know every detail.

"So, you got to Mark's house, then what?"

"I went inside, and I found the gun, then I saw his body. Jesus, man, there was so much blood..."

"Go back," Screech said calmly. "Was the door unlocked?"

"No—wait, it must have been. I don't have a key and Mark wasn't answering the door."

"Any other cars in the driveway? On the street?"

"On the driveway, no, but the street? Fuck, I dunno. I was shaking pretty bad. Surprised I didn't hit somebody on the way."

In his periphery, Screech saw Leroy cringe.

Not a great choice of words.

"Okay, so you open the door and head inside... then what? Did you see the body right away?"

Brock shook his head.

"No, I saw the gun on the counter first. I don't even know why I picked it—'prolly 'cuz I was just so scared. The whole time, I'm calling out Mark's name, but there's no answer. So, I walked into the family room and that's when I saw his body. He was lying on the floor, face down, his head all fucked up—blood everywhere. So, just like at MSG, I ran. Came right here."

Screech thought about this sequence of events for a moment. Hanna started to say something, but he hushed her.

She wasn't happy about it, but her jaw snapped shut, nonetheless.

"How do you know that Mark is dead?" he asked bluntly.

Brock made a face.

"How? What do you mean, *how*? Did you not hear me? His head was all messed up and there was blood everywhere."

"Did you touch his body? Feel for a pulse? Start chest compressions?"

"What? No, I didn't touch his fucking body." Brock was starting to get angry now, which was good. It showed that while he was shocked and frightened, he was also angry that all this shit had gone down.

That was good, because it was normal if such a thing as normal existed in situations such as these.

"Why'd you take the gun, Brock?"

"What is this? Why you grillin' me?"

"Just answer the question."

Hanna suddenly reached out and touched the back of his arm.

"Screech, maybe—"

He shook her off.

"What, you think this is bad? What do you think the cops are gonna do when they have you locked in a room for three days? Huh?" Screech turned back to Brock. "You came to me, remember? If you want us to help, just answer the questions."

Brock's eye that was still able to open all the way blazed into Screech, but eventually, the man shook his head and sighed.

"I took the gun 'cuz I was scared, aight? I was scared because someone just fuckin' killed my manager. I didn't know if he was still in the house, or if he was out to get me, or whatever. That's why I took the gun."

Screech nodded.

"And you didn't fire it?"

"No, I didn't fire it. Jesus."

"What about with your homies last week? You fire some shots in the air? Do some target practice in the woods?"

Brock pushed away from the table but fell short of rising to his feet.

"The fuck?" he looked at Leroy, who just shrugged. "The *homies*?"

"Brock, just answer the question," Hanna implored.

"No," Brock replied through clenched teeth. "No, I didn't fire this gun or any other. I've never fired a damn gun."

Screech let some of the tension out of his shoulders.

"Good, good."

A silence fell over the table, during which time Screech sipped his now lukewarm coffee.

Eventually, Brock spoke up again, his tone calmer now.

"Well, what do we do now?"

"*We* don't do anything," Screech answered. "But *you* are going to turn yourself in."

Screech expected Brock to protest, but he was broken and bruised.

"If you think that's best, I'll do it."

"But you're going to keep your mouth shut. You know what you did when I asked you questions? Got all mad? You're not going to do that with the cops. You are going to remain quiet. I'm going to get a lawyer—on your tab—and he's going to do the talking for you. Do you understand?"

"Yeah. I get it. Keep my mouth shut. What about the gun?"

Screech's eyes drifted to the handgun on Hanna's desk.

"You let us deal with that. Don't mention the gun. Not to anyone."

Brock nodded.

"Normally, the cops can only hold you for twenty-four hours before pressing charges. I'm guessing, though, given how high profile this case is going to be, they'll probably petition a judge to stretch it to two days, maybe three. Can you keep quiet for three days?"

"As long as it takes, man. If you tell me that becoming a fuckin' monk will help you find who did this to Mark and Shane, I'll do it—I'll do anything."

Like maybe not *pick up the probable murder weapon and bring it here?*

And yet, despite this reactionary thought, Screech believed the man before him was telling the truth.

There were few careers more alpha than a professional fighter, and yet Brock had already cried twice and had literally spilled his feelings on the table.

Still, there was one more thing that Screech had to say before he called Brock a lawyer.

"So far, you've been straight with me, so I'll be straight with you." He paused for effect, but when no one intervened,

Screech continued. "Brock, if you had anything to do with Mark's or Shane's death, outside of what I saw on that video, it would be in your best interest to just get up and walk away. I'll wait ten minutes, then call the cops and give them the gun. I won't tell them a single word about what you said here tonight."

Brock started to shake his head, but Screech wasn't done yet.

"Because if I dig up some evidence to the contrary, that proves you were lying to me? I'll be the first one to go to the cops. And unlike you, I won't be keeping my mouth shut. I'll tell them everything. Do you understand?"

Chapter 12

SCREECH COULDN'T STAND LOOKING at Roger Schneiderman's smug face for one second longer, and he couldn't believe that he was doing business with the man again.

But Schneiderman had managed to finagle Drake out of a sticky situation, as well as resolve the Greta Armatridge mess. He was also the only lawyer that Screech knew.

"I've gotta say, I was very surprised to see your number pop up on my call display. At two in the morning, no less," Roger said, with a wry grin.

Screech debated punching him then, giving up everything and going to jail for assault. It might've even been worth it. Thankfully, Hanna stepped forward. What a day it must have been for her to be the coolheaded one.

"Yeah, well, just be grateful that we keep throwing business your way."

Roger raised an eyebrow and turned to her.

"I'm going to pretend that you didn't just say that, given the fact that you still owe me two months' retainer."

"I think this more than makes up for it, don't you? You get Brock Page off, and you no longer have to rely on us to provide you with clients... they'll come running."

Roger shot a glance over his shoulder at Brock, who was seated near the door, his hands in his lap, his head hung low. For a moment, Screech thought he was sleeping. But then he looked up, startled, then went back to his original pose.

Screech got the impression based on his demeanor that Brock might not sleep again for some time. Shit, he might not sleep again until he was either behind bars or they figured out who was behind all this.

"All right, we'll call it a wash then. At least I know that Brock over there is going to pay his bills. What's our angle here, anyway? Is he pleading insanity?" Roger made a twirling gesture around his temple with a finger. "PTSD or TBI... something like that?"

"That's your call, but I don't think he did it. How long do you think they're going to keep him before pressing charges?"

"Well, based on what I know, the DA is going to try to combine Shane's murder with Mark's, that's a given. Seventy-two hours, tops. You know, New York loves to prop up its superstars, but you know what they like more?"

Screech shook his head. He didn't know, and he didn't care. He just wanted to get some rest, clear his head, and start digging tomorrow.

"Bringing them down—they love to see the rich and famous fall. Seeing that it's the weekend, they probably won't get Brock in front of a judge until Monday morning."

"What about bail?" Screech asked although he thought he already knew the answer.

"Unlikely."

Screech took a moment to try and figure out how to broach the next subject. In the end, he went with obtuse.

"And what if they can't find the murder weapon? Let's say it's *misplaced* for a while."

Very subtle, Screech.

Roger saw right through him.

"You mean what are the implications for Brock or for the party that 'finds' the gun?"

"Both."

"It's better for Brock if they *never* find it. But let's say the gun was found later and it comes to light that it had been handed over to a respectable PI. Let's also assume that some semblance of a chain of custody was maintained."

When the man didn't continue, Screech held his hands out expectantly.

"Yeah? And?"

"Then I'd imagine that this might be… overlooked."

Bravo, Roger—all the subtlety of a nymphomaniac in a whorehouse.

Clearly, *overlooked* meant probably not charged with obstruction.

"Okay, do your thing then. Take him in."

Roger Schneiderman nodded and held out his hand.

Screech stared it at for several moments, unable to prevent the sneer that curled his upper lip.

I'm turning into Drake. I'm turning into a younger, thinner, less alcoholic Drake, making enemies of everyone, everywhere I go.

He reluctantly shook the lawyer's hand and walked him to the door. Brock nodded at him, and together he and the lawyer stepped into the hallway.

Before closing the door, however, Screech added one more thing.

"Oh, and if you see a Sergeant Yasiv hanging around? It's probably best that you not mention me or this PI firm. A Detective Dunbar, on the other hand, might be able to help you out."

Roger Schneiderman gave him a look.

"You know Sergeant Yasiv?"

"We go back a ways. But let's just say we had a falling out recently."

Something crossed over Roger's face—something other than self-satisfaction. Screech wanted nothing more than to have the man out of his sight, but he felt compelled to ask what this was all about.

"What? You know him?"

"Of him," Schneiderman said slowly. "You really have a knack for fraternizing with would be murderers, you know that? First Drake, then Yasiv, then Mr. Page here." He slapped Brock on the back, but the man barely seemed to notice.

Screech frowned.

"First of all, Drake didn't kill anybody and, second— wait, *what*? What did you say about Sergeant Yasiv?"

"You didn't hear? Your buddy from the 62nd precinct is up for murder."

Screech couldn't believe what he was hearing and shook his head.

"Sergeant Yasiv… Sergeant Henry Yasiv? Tall guy, smokes a ton of cigarettes? Came up around the same time Drake left the NYPD?"

Roger nodded.

"Yeah, looks like the good Sergeant killed two people in South Carolina… I've heard rumors that they're also going to charge him with the murder of that army vet… Captain Brandon Loomis. Have you been living under a rock or something?"

PART II

Homicide

Chapter 13

LEROY TOOK A DEEP breath as he stared up at Pike's boxing gym. It was an intimidating place, especially to him. Never a fighter, Leroy had watched his brother get shot and killed right in front of him, and all he could do was run.

And now he was here, at a boxing gym of all places, put to task by Screech and Hanna to try and find out whatever he could about Brock Page and Shane Nolasco. The cherry on top would be to figure out how Mark Magnusson, who had been discovered in his home with a single bullet to the head mere hours ago, became entangled in this web of murder.

Leroy was apprehensive—no, he was downright scared. But he was driven by the fact that they all had a role to play in SLH Investigations, and this just happened to be his.

He'd joked that the only reason he was sent here was because he was black, but this time, there was more to it than that. This time, he'd been given this job because he knew the area, the people, and could relate. Thankfully, this time he didn't have to take on a stupid persona and instead could just be plain old Leroy Walker.

And yet, he had a sinking feeling in the pit of his stomach that this was not going be as easy as it looked. Leroy had had the same inclination when he was posing as C.J. Yabooty at the Loomis estate, and look how that turned out.

Still, he was determined, and as the youngest and least experienced member of SLH Investigations, Leroy had to prove his worth.

After another deep breath, Leroy strode forward, placed a hand on the battered metal door of Pike's Boxing gym, and then stepped inside.

The first thing that struck him was the smell. It smelled like every other gym he'd visited in the past, which granted, was few and far between: sweat and exertion. The latter was almost palpable, the odor of power being generated, of calories burned.

The second thing he noticed was the paltry interior. Pike's was at best a glorified warehouse with heavy bags hanging by chains from the ceiling. There were also speed bags off to one side, and a worn-looking boxing ring in the center. Leroy counted six black youths either skipping or pounding fists, including two people sparring in the ring.

Leroy's eyes were drawn to a small office near the back, which was framed by a large window covered in old newspapers as if blinds were a luxury that couldn't be afforded.

Keeping his head low, he started in the direction of the office, observing the motivational quotes that were pasted to the otherwise bare walls as he walked.

He'd almost made it there when someone from the ring hollered out to him.

"Hey kid? You a member here?"

Leroy turned to look at one of the boxers in the ring. He wore padded headgear and in the palm of his boxing glove was a large red mouthpiece.

"No, not yet, anyway. Who should I talk to if I want to become one?"

The man gave him a not-so-subtle once over.

"*You* want to become a member?"

Among other things.

"Maybe."

The boxer turned his eyes to one of the men who was skipping.

"Then you gotta talk to Carl."

With that, he popped his mouthpiece back in, bashed his gloves together, and gestured to his combatant to resume their sparring.

Leroy had been wrong; not all the people in the gym were youths. The man skipping, while in good shape, was probably in his early fifties, if the crow's feet around his eyes were any indication. The man was staring at him, but he made no effort to stop his exercise even when Leroy approached.

Carl, if that's who this man was, sported a cut-off shirt revealing muscular arms that glistened with sweat. He was bald with a thin mustache shading his upper lip and had a skin tone that was lighter than Brock's but not as light as Leroy himself.

Their eyes met, but there was an awkward minute or so when the man seemed content with continuing to skip leaving Leroy to just stand there like a dolt.

Eventually, Carl put down the rope, picked up a towel at his feet and dabbed his forehead.

"You want a membership?"

"Yeah, maybe, but maybe we can just talk first? Think we can go to your office?"

The man frowned.

I knew this wasn't going to be easy.

The police had yet to come here, if they ever would, but Leroy surmised that every single person in Pike's had heard about what had happened at MSG.

Shit, they'd probably talked about it all morning.

"You're too young to be reporter and you're too skinny to be a boxer. Which means you probably got one of those blog things... am I right?"

Leroy looked around hesitantly, aware that everyone had stopped what they were doing to stare at him.

Why do I always get stuck with these jobs? Hanna gets to traipse around in expensive clothes, and I get stuck trying to pry information from sweaty meatheads.

He sighed.

"No, I'm not a blogger, but I do have some questions for you... questions that might be more appropriate for your office. Can we talk in there?"

Carl's frown deepened.

"Hard pass."

Leroy shrugged.

Suit yourself.

"I have a couple of questions about Brock, but, like you said, I'm not a reporter. I'm a PI."

The man stopped wiping his forehead and stared at him, incredulous.

"*You*? A PI? What's that stand for? Primarily Incompetent? Because there's no way that you're a private investigator."

Leroy expected this response and quickly produced a business card.

Carl snatched it from him with lightning speed and brought it close to his face.

"Probably a fake," he mumbled under his breath. Then he turned the card and held it up for the young man in the ring to see. "Hey T-bone, you feel this guy? He says he's a private investigator."

"I *am* a private investigator," Leroy confirmed, but it was apparent that he was only a spectator in this part of the conversation.

"And I'm Mo Ali," the man in the ring shot back.

Carl tapped the card against his palm for a moment before thrusting it back at Leroy.

He nearly dropped it.

"Okay, kid, I'll tell you what. You step in the ring, spar a little, then I'll answer your questions."

Leroy had to fight the urge to roll his eyes.

"I'm not much of a fighter and I'm afraid if I stepped into the ring with you, the only question I'd be able to ask is which way to the nearest hospital. I was hired by Brock, and I need—"

Carl shook his head.

"No, not me, you procrastinating imbecile—Junior."

Leroy didn't care for the insult, but he commended the man for keeping with the theme. He also didn't want to look around but couldn't help himself.

Leroy half expected that 'Junior' was one of those ironic nicknames and that a hulking giant of a man who made George Foreman look like Tyrion Lannister to come lumbering out of the shadows.

But no one stepped forward.

"Who's Junior?" Leroy blurted. As soon as the words exited his mouth, he wished he could take them back. Because he knew how Carl would interpret them, and the man didn't disappoint: a grin formed on his face.

"C'mon, Junior."

There was a kid who looked about all of eleven years old filling a water bottle off to one side. At the mention of his name, he stopped what he was doing and strutted over. At just over five feet tall and eighty-five pounds with cement shoes on, Junior was far from an intimidating sight.

"I'm Junior, motherfucker, best you remember that. You want step in the fucking ring with me nigga? You wanna bang it out? Cuz Imma fuck you up, son."

Chapter 14

"THIS IS A GOOD thing… right?" Hanna asked tentatively.

Screech could only stare at the computer screen in disbelief. Somehow, he'd managed to push all of this out of his mind the night prior. Either he'd been too distracted by the whole Brock Page clusterfuck or exhaustion had just taken hold. But now…

"How is this… how is this possible?" Screech asked, ignoring Hanna's question.

What Roger had told him about Sergeant Henry Yasiv was true. The man had been charged with the murder of Alister and Holly Cameron of South Carolina. What's more, is that the NYPD were also investigating him for another murder, a local victim. Although no names were mentioned, every person with a computer and twitter account were screaming that this victim was Captain Brandon Loomis.

Screech started to shake.

"I have no idea," Hanna said with a shrug. "But at least that means he won't be coming around here harassing us anymore."

"But… but Yasiv didn't kill Loomis, I—"

If Hanna hadn't stopped him then, Screech might have said something that he would regret.

She reached down and grabbed him so tightly by the shoulders that he actually cried out.

"Don't say it. Don't you fucking say it. Whatever you did or didn't do, it was because you were protecting us—me, Jasmine, Leroy. But don't you fucking say it, Screech."

Hanna was glaring at him so intently, that Screech wasn't sure if she was angry or—

"The gun," he nearly gasped. "The fucking gun!"

Screech shook free of her grip and dropped to his knees. The holster was still strapped to the underside of his desk, but like the night prior, it was empty.

"It's not just going to magically appear, Screech. Are you sure you put it back there?"

Screech nodded, but then stopped.

Did I put it there?

Last night, he'd been positive. And a gun, a murder weapon, wasn't something you just 'misplaced' like the TV remote.

Then where the fuck is it?

"I'll find it," Hanna said. "I'll find the goddamn gun, Screech. But in the meantime, we only have three days to figure out what happened to Shane Nolasco and Mark Magnusson. That needs to be our focus, now."

Screech had no idea how she could compartmentalize something like this, but Hanna was nothing if not persistent.

"Screech? You need to snap the fuck out of it."

"Sorry," he managed. "What... what should we do?"

The question was purposefully ambiguous; Screech hoped that Hanna would address both present matters that dealt with potential incarceration and was grateful when she started rooting around in her desk.

But when she returned with Brock Page's cell phone in hand, it was clear that her mind was on the boxer's fate and not his.

"What are you doing? What are you looking for?"

Hanna shrugged.

"I dunno—texts, phone calls, anything like that. But it looks like our man Brock was focusing on the fight for the last week or so—unless he has another cell phone he isn't telling us about. The only calls are from his manager, and the only text is the one telling him to come to his house late last night."

As Hanna continued to search, Screech fell into thought.

If Yasiv is being charged with murder… what evidence could they possibly have on him?

Alister and Holly Cameron…

For some reason, the Cameron surname resonated with him and he punched it into Google. When the first image popped up of a large man wearing a dark robe, Screech felt as if he'd been punched in the stomach.

"Oh no," he gasped.

Now he knew why the name sounded familiar. It was because he'd seen it before, in the newspaper a while back.

A newspaper that had been on Dr. Beckett Campbell's desk, and the photograph of Reverend Cameron had been defaced with red ink.

No, it can't be, he thought almost desperately. *It* can't *be.*

Screech shut his eyes so tightly that he saw stars. When the stars faded, the universe was replaced be the ocean, and he found himself looking at Donnie DiMarco.

At the time, Screech had been commissioned to find B-*Yacht'ch*, a stolen yacht. Oh, he'd found it alright, and the man who'd stolen it, Donnie DiMarco, had met a watery demise.

Later, the man who'd hired him to find the yacht, Bob Bumacher, had befallen a similarly grisly fate.

As had Craig Sloan long before him.

And now, Reverend Alister Cameron and his wife Holly were dead.

A little digging revealed that the couple were accused of trapping sickly young adults in their basement, using them in some sort of religious scam.

Screech drew a full breath.

Everything pointed back to Beckett, but Screech found himself unable to accept what the evidence was screaming in his face.

"Screech?"

Screech's eyes snapped open and he found a concerned-looking Hanna staring at him.

"You gotta get over this—you did what you had to do to protect us. All of us."

Even though he was looking at Hanna, his mind was still elsewhere.

Could it be? Could Dr. Beckett Campbell, head ME for New York State, the man who helped us out countless times. Including most recently with Greta Armatridge, be a murderer?

It dawned on him that when Yasiv had paid him a visit a while back, he wasn't looking at Screech for Loomis's murder as he'd thought, but at Beckett.

How did I not see this earlier? How could—

"Screech, wake the fuck up!"

Screech finally snapped out of it and he observed Hanna who was holding Brock's cell phone out for him to see.

"Wh—what'd you find?"

Hanna stared at him for several moments before answering, just in case he was compelled to fall back into thought.

"It looks like Brock was seeing someone on the side," she said bluntly. "Someone who definitely wasn't his manager."

"Really? Who?"

Hanna pushed the phone closer to his face, and Screech squinted at the small screen.

"Dr. Linda Fremont? Who the hell is that? Physiotherapist? Trainer?"

Hanna shook her head, a grin forming on her lips.

"Sport's Psychiatrist."

Screech frowned.

"Why are you smiling?"

"Because, Screech, if there's anybody who knew what was going on in Brock Page's head before that fight, it's gonna be his psychiatrist, don't you think?"

Screech followed along, but he didn't share her apparent optimism.

"Sure, but there's no way that she's going to talk to us. Shit, they won't even talk to the cops."

"No, you're right."

"And… you're still smiling."

"Yep—because you're right; this Dr. Fremont would never talk to Hanna from SLH Investigations. But she will talk to Natalia Abramovsky."

Tired and emotionally exhausted, Screech just shook his head.

"Who the hell is Natalia Abramovsky?"

Hanna suddenly rose to her feet and stood adroitly.

"Why, Natalia is a struggling Russian tennis star," she said in a thick Baltic accent. "One that is in desperate need of psychiatric help."

Chapter 15

"NO WAY—I'M NOT fighting him," Leroy said, shaking his head. "There's no way."

"That's because you're a chicken shit motherfucker," Junior replied.

Leroy continued to shake his head in disbelief—both at the proposition and at the eleven-year-old's language.

"Then you're not getting anything from me, not about Brock, anyway," Carl said, starting to dab the sweat from his brow again. "And watch your language, Junior."

This is ridiculous.

"He's just a kid; I'm not fighting him. I'm not fighting anybody. Brock hired me to help him, and I thought you'd be on board."

"Why would I want to help Brock?" Carl asked.

"Because he used to train here? Because—"

"You don't want to fight me, because you're a chicken shit," Junior interjected. "A little pussy. Cracker talkin', silver spoon, nigga. Where you live? Fifth Avenue?"

Frustrated now, Leroy turned to Junior and glowered at him.

"You've got a filthy mouth, you know that?"

"It's from eating your mom's—"

Without thinking, Leroy stepped forward and reached for the boy. Junior swatted his hand away.

"What did I tell you about that mouth?" Carl barked.

Junior shrugged, but never took his eyes off Leroy.

"Listen, Leroy, if you're not going to box…" Carl let his sentence trail off.

Leroy felt squeezed, but he was wholly uninterested in this game.

He held up his hands.

"Okay, fine."

He was about to leave it at that when Junior had one more thing to say, the only thing that Leroy was unable to ignore.

"Looks like the wrong Walker boy was shot, wouldn't you say?"

Leroy saw red.

He had no idea how this little shit knew about Declan, or if he'd gotten lucky with his stream of consciousness insults.

Either way, it didn't matter.

He looked briefly to Carl, who had since resumed skipping.

"All right," Leroy said in a flat tone, facing Junior again. "You want to step in the cage with me? Let's do this then. I'm gonna enjoy wiping that grin off your face."

***

Once the gloves were strapped on and the headgear in place—both of which were too large—Leroy felt more than ridiculous. And staring across the ring at a foul-mouthed eleven-year-old made him feel like some sort of abusive stepfather.

How in the world did I get myself into this mess?

Leroy felt like tearing everything off and just heading back to Screech empty-handed.

But another part of him actually wanted to smack some sense into the boy, if only for a moment. Oh, and there was the promise of information about Brock, too.

Win, win, win…

"So, just three minutes, right?" he said over his shoulder. Everyone in the gym had gathered around, hanging their arms over the ropes and staring at him as if he were insane.

Carl produced a digital clock and set it on the apron of the ring. It showed three minutes in large red letters.

"Three minutes, starting now," Carl informed them, clicking a button at the top of the clock.

There was no bell, at least. That would've pushed the absurdity to another level.

Leroy stepped forward, holding his gloves up as he'd seen Brock do during his short fight.

Junior was less conventional; he fluttered his feet, a throwback to Mohammed Ali, and then came out twirling his gloves.

Annoyed by this, Leroy threw the first punch: an anemic jab.

Junior easily dodged the blow, and then brought his hands up in a more traditional stance.

"Come on, you pussy," he taunted.

Leroy threw another half-hearted jab, and Junior parried to his right.

"That all you got?"

Leroy went to throw a third consecutive punch, but he'd only started to extend his arm before something hit him in the side. It wasn't a particularly hard blow, but it stung, and he instinctively lowered his elbow to protect his kidney.

Junior jumped backward and did the fluttery thing with his feet again.

Jesus, he's fast, Leroy thought.

"Come on, come on, now. Imma make you my bitch."

Knowing that he had to take things more seriously, instead of seeing the kid in front of him, Leroy pictured the thug who'd shot his brother. The man had since been killed by corrupt cops, but that didn't matter.

He tried to cut off the ring, but this only served to tire him out.

The thug slid quickly across the canvas, seeming to know Leroy's movements even before he did.

"Hey, if I beat you, can I get that chain from around your neck? You can keep the big D—I bet you like that sorta thing—but the chain? No? Prolly plastic, anyway."

My chain...?

Leroy had forgotten all about the chain that hung around his neck, the one that had belonged to his brother, Declan. It wasn't plastic, but 18 karat gold, the initial and the chain both.

Maybe that's how he knew that I had a brother. After all, I said my name was Leroy and this is a 'D'. He probably just guessed—

Junior stepped forward and delivered a straight jab. Leroy wasn't expecting the punch, and his hands spread upon impact. While the blow was mostly absorbed by the padded headgear, his head still flew back awkwardly. Out of instinct, Leroy fired back, but Junior was no longer standing in front of him.

"Fuck," he grumbled, turning to his left.

"So? You having fun yet?" the boy taunted.

Leroy took two aggressive steps forward, but while he was flat-footed, Junior was on his toes. The kid leaped to his right and delivered another blow to his kidney, this one significantly harder than the first. When Leroy predictably lowered his elbow, Junior struck him squarely in the jaw with a left.

Stars scattered across his vision, and in his inexperience, he reached out with both hands to try to clinch up. In doing so, Leroy's face was exposed, and that's when Junior went full out attack mode.

Leroy didn't know how many punches were landed — it could have been anywhere between three and one hundred. Disoriented, he staggered forward, which caused his chin to jut out.

A well-placed uppercut brought Leroy to a knee.

Even though he was struggling to catch his breath, he saw Junior coming toward him, and he held up a hand to try and fend him off.

I'm going to die. I'm going to die at the hands of an eleven-year-old brat.

Someone clapped, and Junior stopped advancing.

"That's enough, Junior," Carl said as he stepped into the ring.

"Bro, you couldn't even last thirty seconds."

Leroy, finally able to draw a full breath, rested one arm on the ropes and tried to pull himself to his feet. But his midsection cried out in pain and he dropped back down again. As he did, his eyes fell to the clock which had been stopped at two minutes and thirty-four seconds.

The boy was right. He hadn't even lasted thirty seconds.

Carl walked over to Junior and patted him on the shoulder.

"Good stuff, Junior. Now I want you to do twenty laps of the gym."

The boy's eyes went wide.

"What? What the fuck for? I dusted his ass. Nigga didn't even land a single punch."

Carl scowled.

"Because of that mouth of yours, that's why. Now do it."

Junior looked as if he was about to say something, but then bowed his head and left the ring, leaving behind a trail of mumbles.

Carl went to Leroy next and helped him to his feet.

"I wouldn't feel too bad about it; the kid comes from a pretty solid pedigree."

Leroy winced as the man removed his gloves and then his headgear. His jaw hurt, but his stomach ached. He felt like he'd been stepped on by a three-hundred-pound man, not clubbed by a seventy-pound kid.

"All right," he said, in a strained voice. "I played your game. Now you have to answer my questions about Brock."

Carl threw his head back and laughed.

"Yeah, fat chance of that."

"What? What do you mean? You said —"

Carl gripped his shoulder tightly.

"I don't care who hired you — Brock, Shane, or Mike Tyson. We don't talk to outsiders."

Leroy was incredulous.

"That's —"

Leroy stopped speaking when Carl pointed at Junior who was in the process of removing his boxing gloves. The implication was simple, yet effective: keep talking and I'll set my dog on you again.

"Whatever," Leroy snapped. Even if Carl swore a blood oath that he'd spill the beans about Brock, he wasn't stepping into the ring with that little psycho again.

If Screech wants the information that bad, he can challenge Junior Mohammad Ali… or is it Mohammad Ali Jr.? I've taken enough of a beating for one day.

Chapter 16

HANNA WASN'T SURPRISED TO find Dr. Linda Fremont's practice in the Upper East Side. Located in a one-story commercial complex, the clinic, aptly named Sport Brain, was sandwiched between an insurance company and a real estate headquarters. Figuring that her small Volkswagen would be out of place in the lot, she parked across the street. Besides, Natalia Abramovsky would never be seen driving a VW.

After smoothing her blouse and skirt—both of which still had the tags on, to be returned later—she practiced her gait as she crossed the street.

Just before entering the building, she slipped on a pair of over-sized Maui Jim sunglasses.

Hanna kept her head held high as she entered Sport Brain but used her periphery to scope the place out. There was a row of seats on one side and a table littered with sports magazines in front of it. A lonely water cooler was located on the other side of the door.

Her focus, however, was on the young blonde woman sitting behind an over-sized desk square in the center of the room. She was attractive, clearly appealing to a specific clientele.

"Hello," Hanna said in a thick Russian accent.

"Hi there, how may I help you?" the perky blonde said with a smile. She was wearing a blue top that, while it gave the appearance of being a designer brand, was a fake. A good fake, but a fake nonetheless.

"I'm here to see Dr. Fremont," Hanna said bluntly.

The blonde's smile didn't falter, but she did bat her eyelashes.

"Let me just check," she said. Her fingers danced over the keyboard, and Hanna noted that while the ring finger of her left hand had the indentations of a ring, she wasn't wearing one.

Already, an impression of Sport Brain was beginning to form in her mind, and it wasn't a good one.

"I'm sorry, but Dr. Fremont doesn't have any appointments this afternoon in her calendar."

Hanna nodded.

"Good. She shall be able to see me, then."

"No, what I mean is that we will have to schedule an appointment for another time. We don't do walk-ins here at Sport Brain. What did you say your name was?"

Hanna lifted her chin.

"I didn't. But you say you have no appointments today. That is good. I need to see her."

The woman shook her head.

"I'm sorry, but that just won't be possible. Next week, maybe, but that—"

Hanna placed her palms on the woman's desk and leaned forward.

"I am Natalia Abramovsky and I need to see Dr. Fremont today."

The name meant nothing to the woman, of course; Hanna had just made it up. But she knew that privileged athlete such as the one she was portraying wouldn't leave without seeing the doctor or making a scene.

"Well, Natalia, as I said, I can book you in for next week. But unfortunately, Dr. Fremont cannot see you today."

"That's not good enough. I have a tournament next week. I need to see her today."

As she spoke, Hanna reached into her clutch, a knock-off Coach bag, and pulled out a wad of bills. It was only five hundred bucks in twenties, but she had folded it back on itself twice and wrapped it in an elastic to make it look like more.

"Today—I see her today."

Hanna was happy to see that the woman's eyes were locked on the money, but she resisted the urge to take it.

"I'm sorry, I really am, but—"

The door at the end of the hall suddenly opened and a burly man in a blue polo walked out, clipboard in hand.

The man strode with purpose towards the front door, but Hanna wasn't so much interested in him as the woman behind him. Standing in the office was a petite woman with blond hair pulled into a bun, hands locked on her hips. Like the secretary, she was young and pretty, with full lips and large eyes that almost appeared caged behind dark glasses.

"Jordyn, I need you to—" the woman, whom Hanna was almost certain was Dr. Fremont, stopped when she noticed her. "Who's this?"

"My name is Natalia Abramovsky and I need to see you."

"Jordyn?" Dr. Fremont said.

"Yes, I told Mrs. Abrama—I told *her* that you weren't seeing any patients, but she—"

"I need to see you today, Dr. Fremont," Hanna interrupted, holding up the cash.

The woman's eyes followed the money.

"You want me to call security, Dr. Fremont?"

A tight smile appeared on the doctor's lips. Then she took one hand off her hip and gestured to the office behind her.

"No, that's all right, Jordyn, I think I can maybe squeeze in a quick session if she's paying cash. What did you say your name was again?"

Chapter 17

SCREECH MANAGED TO GET past the line of reporters and protesters by flashing his PI credentials, presumably because the cops were too preoccupied to actually look at it properly. But now, as he neared the entrance to Madison Square Garden, security became even tighter. A high-profile case such as this one, the death of a boxer in the ring, had societal as well as political implications. Case in point the dozens of protesters and paparazzi that he'd already elbowed his way through.

But the line of police officers and detectives suggested that this was the end of the road.

I have to get inside; I have to see where Shane died. I also need to see Brock's boxing gloves.

Although he was no expert, there was something about the way that Shane's neck snapped back with each punch that seemed wholly unnatural.

"I'm sorry, police only," a stern-looking NYPD officer said as Screech approached the yellow tape.

Screech pulled out his PI badge and flashed it to the officer, hoping that he wouldn't inspect it too closely. He got as far as lifting the tape, when the man put a hand on the center of his chest, stopping his forward advance.

"Let me see that badge again," he demanded.

Screech begrudgingly held his badge out. The officer took a long look, then shook his head.

"Police only," he repeated.

Screech cursed under his breath.

"I've been hired by Brock Page—I'm a private investigator. I need to get in there, I need to see the scene."

The officer was unimpressed.

"Police only."

Desperate now, Screech got on his toes and tried to peer past the man. As he did, two other officers joined the first.

"This guy giving you problems, Bernie?" a younger version of the first officer asked.

"I dunno, you gonna give me trouble, PI-man?"

It was almost as if they were looking for a fight. Or anything to do, really.

Screech wasn't going to give them the satisfaction. Just as he turned to leave, however, he spotted a familiar face on the other side of the tape.

"Dunbar!" he hollered, waving his hand.

"Nice try, buddy, but you're not getting in there. Now step away from the tape."

Screech ignored him and waved his arm more vigorously.

"Dunbar!"

"All right, that's enough," Bernie said, reaching for his arm. In an instant, Screech's wrist was behind his back, pushed up nearly to his shoulder blade.

"If you resist, I'll throw you in jail. We've already tossed three paparazzi in County," the man hissed in his ear, inching his arm up even further. Pain started to radiate from his upper arm, but Screech remained rooted

"Detective Dunbar!"

"Just throw him in the back of the van with the others, Bernie."

"Hold on. Jesus, gimme—"

"Screech?"

Bernie turned around to face the approaching man but didn't release his hold on Screech's wrist.

"You know this man, Detective?"

Detective Dunbar, who looked as if he'd aged ten years since the last time Screech had seen him, nodded.

"Yeah, I know him. Let him go, let him through."

Bernie pushed Screech's arm up just a little higher before releasing him.

"My bad."

Wincing, Screech shook out his arm and then stepped under the tape, fighting the urge to shoot the officers who'd stopped him a look.

He didn't need any more enemies.

"Screech," Dunbar said, lowering his voice and glancing around nervously. "What the hell are you doing here? Is it… is it Drake?"

Screech shook his head.

"No, it's not Drake. It's Brock Page… I need to get inside, Dunbar. I need to see where Shane was killed."

Chapter 18

WITH BOTH HIS PRIDE and body wounded, Leroy collected his things and started out of the gym. He was frustrated beyond belief and annoyed that he'd been lied to. But he didn't blame Carl. After all, he was from this neighborhood, too, from their world. And in this world, the police weren't preventative, they were reactionary and punitive. Their job was to put someone behind bars. Although Leroy wasn't the police, he was a PI, which might even be worse.

As he stepped outside, a hand came down on his shoulder.

"Leroy?"

Leroy spun around, half-expecting to be pummeled by Junior again or verbally berated by Carl. But instead, it was one of the other boxers, a man in his mid-twenties who hadn't said a word up to now.

"Yeah?" Leroy asked tentatively, taking a step backward just in case the man felt like finishing the job that Junior started.

"My name's Jamaal," the man said, also cautiously leaning away.

"And my name's Leroy."

"Yeah, I know."

The two men stared at each other for a few moments, before Jamaal adjusted the bag slung over one shoulder and said, "Wanna grab a coffee or something?"

Leroy was hesitant but eventually nodded.

After all, things couldn't get worse than being pummeled by an eleven-year-old punk in front of a crowd, could it?

"Yeah, sure, why not?"

***

"You don't remember me, do you?" Jamaal asked as he stared down at his cup of coffee. Leroy had ordered a latte but had no intention of drinking it.

He was jittery enough as it was.

"No, sorry. It's been a busy and crazy last six months or so."

Jamaal nodded.

"I knew your brother. I knew Declan."

Leroy's eyes went wide.

"You did?"

He didn't know all of Declan's friends, but this man, this athlete, didn't seem like the kind of person that his brother would hang out with.

That was reserved for more shady characters of the type their mother would never approve.

"I was his friend a long time ago. But I always liked your brother and I'm sorry about what happened to him. I was going to go to the funeral, but…" the man let his sentence to trail off. "Well, I'm sorry about what happened to him."

Leroy hadn't thought of his brother lately, despite the fact that the chain he wore around his neck was a constant reminder. What he would never forget, however, was his promise that he would get out. And he had gotten out, in his own way. Not the way that Declan nor his mother had wanted, but Leroy had found his own path. A path that had led him to Drake and Screech and Hanna and to him becoming part of something… and he wanted to keep it that way.

"Thanks. It was fucked up."

Jamaal looked about to say something, and then instead sipped his coffee.

Leroy had a feeling that Jamaal had more to say, but his instincts told him not to press.

Eventually, Jamaal started to open up.

"You know, I was into some of the stuff that Leroy was into when we were in high school... shady characters, smoking too much weed, that sort of thing. But then I found boxing, and things changed. After that, we didn't really talk much anymore. Listen, I heard you say that you're a private investigator or something? How old are you, if you don't mind me asking?"

"Almost nineteen."

"So how does a kid like you from the ghetto become a private investigator? No offense, of course."

Leroy wasn't offended. He *was* just a kid from the ghetto after all, and sometimes it was important to remember where you'd come from to appreciate where you were now.

The truth was that becoming a PI had been sheer chance. If it hadn't been for charging home and seeing his mom beat up and then subsequently thrown in jail, he probably would've ended up the same way his brother had. But in prison, he'd met Drake and they'd exchanged favors.

Leroy opted for, "It's a long story. Basically, I wanted to find out what happened to my brother, and one thing led to another..."

"And now Brock... Brock hired you?"

An image of the teary-eyed, battered man came to mind. "Yeah."

"I saw his fight, you know," Jamaal said, once again turning his eyes to his coffee. "We all did—we all watched it. It was fucking crazy. I couldn't believe it—I mean, Brock hasn't knocked anyone out in over a year, and Shane has never been KO'd. TKO'd sure, but not KO'd. Thirty fights, zero KO's. Until last night."

This surprised Leroy.

"Really?"

"Yeah. I wasn't at Pike's when they used to train there, but I met 'em a couple of times." Jamaal lowered his voice an octave. "In fact, they were both in about a week ago."

More surprise.

"Like, together?"

"Uh-huh."

"And is that… normal?"

"No, not at all. I mean, I heard that they were friends back in the day, but before squarin' off at MSG? No fuckin' way. And they were arguing, too."

Leroy leaned forward. He was interested before, but now he was captivated.

"For real? What were they arguing about?"

Jamaal reached in his pocket and pulled out his cell phone.

"The audio is shit, but maybe you can read lips better than I can."

Leroy's eyes bulged.

"You got a video of them?"

Jamaal nodded.

"Nobody knows I have this, and I'm not sure if I should even show you, but what happened to Shane… fuck, here, check it out."

Chapter 19

"**WHAT CAN I HELP** you with, Natalia?" Dr. Fremont asked as she took up residence behind her desk. Hanna slowly made her way to the comfortable chair across from the woman.

"It's my backhand," she said, keeping with the thick Russian accent. "It always goes long. In practice, it lands good, in game, not so much. My forehand? Perfect."

Dr. Fremont eyed her suspiciously for a moment, then her eyes darted to the billfold that Hanna had rested on the desk.

"And when did this start, Natalia? Has this always been an issue or has something happened in your personal life that has affected your game?"

Hanna pursed her lips.

"No, it's not always. It's recent," she said. There was something odd about the way that Dr. Fremont was posing her questions, but Hanna was too busy trying to figure out how to transition to discussing Brock Page to pay this much attention. As she contemplated this, her eyes drifted to the cabinets behind Dr. Fremont, which she presumed contained the woman's notes. "I think it started —"

"Last night? After the boxing match?" Dr. Fremont finished for her.

Clearly, while Hanna had picked up on the woman's subtle glance toward the cash, Dr. Fremont had also noticed her wandering eyes.

"Uhh-excuse me?"

Dr. Fremont's heart-shaped lips turned downward.

"Did this problem with your 'backhand' happen after Shane Nolasco died in the ring last night?"

Hanna tried to feign confusion or surprise, but she knew the gig was up. Still, she gave it the good ol' college try.

"I don't know what you're talking about. I think it was my divorce that affected my—"

"Right, your backhand. Do you think that I'm an idiot, Natalia, or whatever your name is?"

"No, I—"

"I follow tennis, follow the WTA, and I've never heard of a Natalia Abramovsky." Dr. Fremont leaned forward, her frown deepening. "Are you a reporter? Is that it? I think you coming here is deplorable. A man lost his life last night, and another's hangs in the balance. And you're here, what? Playing games? Trying to coax information out of me?"

"I came here for you to fix my head, not fuck with it," Hanna said. She reached out to grab the money, but Dr. Fremont was faster. The cash was out of sight before Hanna's hand even touched the desk.

"My sessions are very expensive, but I think this is going to be your first and only visit, don't you?"

Hanna rose to her feet in a huff.

"You are the worst doctor I have ever seen."

Dr. Fremont was unmoved by the insult.

"Have a nice day, Natalia. Oh, and before you leave, I would think twice about coming back here."

Hanna, who was partway to the door, stopped and leveled an icy stare at the woman behind the desk.

"Why's that?" she asked, dropping the accent entirely now.

"Because if you don't, I'm going to get one of my MMA clients to pay you a visit, see if they can help you with that backhand of yours."

"I'd watch what you say, doctor. Because while my backhand is fucked, my forehand is on point."

With that, Hanna left the office. With every step toward the front door, the smile on her lips grew a little bit wider.

"So, should I book you for another appointment next week?" The blonde behind the desk asked as Hanna passed.

She shook her head.

"You know what? I think that one session will suffice. That boss of yours? She's a real piece of work, you know that?"

Chapter 20

DUNBAR SURPRISED SCREECH BY opening his arms and giving him a big hug. This reaction was so unexpected that Screech actually stumbled. When he collected himself, he slapped the man awkwardly on the back with both hands and then pulled away.

"Am I glad to see you," Dunbar said with a grin.

That's a first, Screech thought.

"Yeah, it's been a while," he replied tentatively.

"Come on, let's go for a walk. I can take you to the ring."

Screech, still confused as to what was going on, followed Dunbar through the maze that was MSG. They passed dozens of uniformed men, all of whom appeared to be doing nothing but standing around. As they neared the entrance to the main arena, Dunbar asked him why he was here, and why he was interested in seeing where Shane had died.

Screech quickly debated his options but was so taken aback by the man's attitude, that he opted for the truth.

"To be honest with you, Dunbar, I was hired by Brock Page to investigate what happened here, at MSG, and at his manager's house."

Dunbar's demeanor immediately changed.

The truth, clearly, hadn't set him free, instead, it had backed him into a corner.

"Seriously?" Dunbar stopped walking and faced Screech. "Brock Page hired you?"

Screech nodded.

"Yeah. I was the one who convinced him to turn himself in."

Dunbar just stared at him for several moments, before shaking his head.

"You… you shouldn't be here."

And here it comes… the stonewalling.

But Dunbar started walking toward the arena again, and Screech eagerly followed.

"First the mayor, and now Brock Page," the detective grumbled. "Even when Drake's not around, bad things just keep happening to those who knew him."

"Speaking of which—"

"Before you ask, there's still nothing I can do about his outstanding warrant."

Screech shook his head.

"No, not that. I was referring to the bad things that happen to his friends… I was referring to Sergeant Yasiv."

Dunbar stopped again but instead of concern on his face, there was something else.

Something that could have been guilt.

"I can't speak of any details, Screech. But what I will say, is that Yasiv made some powerful enemies, enemies that want to see him gone from the force… and maybe even New York. This whole business in South Carolina is probably going to blow over, but that's just the beginning."

"Captain Loomis," Screech whispered without thinking.

Dunbar made a face and held his palms up, reaffirming that he was unable to provide any more information. Maybe that he'd already said too much.

With that, Dunbar led him into the arena, and Screech paused for a second to take it all in. He'd been here before, of course, for numerous Rangers games and a handful of concerts. But during all of his visits, the place had been packed full of screaming fans. Now empty, save for a handful of police officers, the place had lost some of its luster, its mystique.

Considering what had happened here just a few hours ago, it felt more like a gigantic mortuary than a place of worship.

Dunbar started walking toward the ring, and Screech followed.

"What about you, Dunbar? How have you been? Managed to avoid the Drake curse so far?"

He'd meant the comment as a joke, but neither of them found it funny.

"My time in the NYPD is almost up," Dunbar said.

"Really?"

"Yeah, going to be moving over to the SVU. You know, they say that only a special type of person can deal with the atrocities that you'll see in the SVU."

Dunbar paused to lift the ring ropes and allow Screech to step under them.

"But you wanna know what I think?"

Screech stood in the center of the ring and looked around again. MSG may not be the shining spectacle he'd once considered it but staring up at the rows upon rows of empty seats still held a little of the magic that not even the death of Shane Nolasco could take away.

"What's that?"

"I think that what I've seen could give the SVU a run for their money. Corruption, disease, human trafficking, abuse of power, mass suicide, and murder."

Screech couldn't argue with that.

"Speaking of which," Dunbar continued, "you wouldn't happen to know where a particular gun might be? The gun that was used to end Mark Magnusson's life, would you?"

Chapter 21

LEROY FOCUSED ON THE video as Jamaal played it for him a second time.

It clearly showed Shane and Brock, and as Jamaal had indicated, they were arguing about something. And he was telling the truth about the audio, as well; the only thing that Leroy could pick up on was something that sounded like the annoying hum of an air-conditioning unit.

Both men were standing in the office at the back of Pike's Gym. The video was shot through the open door, but while Brock's face was in full view, Shane was mostly standing with his back to the camera. The two men argued for the better part of a minute before it looked as if Brock was about to shove Shane. Shane pulled back and Brock evidently changed his mind.

Then the screen went black.

"Any idea what they were saying?" Leroy asked as Jamaal slipped his cell phone back into his pocket.

"Couldn't hear a word. Carl was skipping right beside me, and there was no way I could get any closer without somebody noticing that I was recording."

So that's what that sound is, Leroy thought, picturing the bald man with his skipping rope.

"What happened after that? Did Shane leave? What about Brock?"

Jamaal nodded.

"Shane took off, kinda bolted out of there, to be honest — looked upset. And then Brock stayed in the office for a while by himself."

"On his phone?"

Jamaal shook his head.

"No; he wasn't doin' nothin'. Just sitting there. Then Carl went in and said a few words. After that, Brock got up and left. Didn't even say goodbye to the other fighters. That's the last time I saw either of them."

Leroy still couldn't wrap his head around why both men were there in the first place. Even if they were paying homage to their old stomping grounds, wouldn't, a week before their fight, somebody—their managers or PR reps—make sure that they weren't there at the same time?

Given that there was no press present, the other possibility was that this wasn't at all about their upcoming bout, but something else entirely

"Jamaal, think you can send me that video? I have some computer software back in the office that might be able to clean up the audio," Leroy said.

Jamaal visibly squirmed.

"Ah, I dunno, Leroy. I feel kinda dirty about this whole thing."

"I'm not trying to embarrass anyone, Jamaal. I'm working for Brock here. You said it yourself, something wasn't right about the fight, about how Shane went down. I just want to know what happened. I'll keep your name out of it."

Jamaal seemed to consider this for several moments before answering.

"Okay, okay. You got one of those cards?"

Leroy pulled out the business card that he'd initially offered to Carl and handed it over. Jamaal stared at it and then, without raising his eyes, said, "You know, not many of us make it out of Tremont, the way you seem to have. It's hard—shit's hard, man."

Ah, there's the ask.

Leroy had come prepared for this—rather, Screech had given him some cash in case wheels needed greasing—and he reached into his pocket and pulled out a hundred-dollar bill.

It was clear that this made Jamaal uneasy, but the man eventually took it.

Leroy didn't blame him.

"Thanks," Jamaal muttered. "I appreciate it, Leroy, I do. But if there's anything else I can do? Something more… permanent? That would be even better."

Leroy nodded.

"Things are tight for us right now, too, Jamaal. But if this works out, if Brock goes free… I'm pretty sure we're gonna need some good people on the streets."

Jamaal's face lit up.

"That's awesome, man. I'll send you the video, but I should get goin'. Got work in an hour."

When Leroy furrowed his brow, Jamaal clarified.

"Baggin' groceries, man."

"Aight, see you soon, bro."

"You too."

Jamaal grabbed his coffee and left Leroy sitting at the table alone.

After about a minute, a smile crept onto Leroy's face. It had been a long time since he'd smiled, and it felt… strange.

Not only had he managed to help someone out, someone from his world, but Screech was going to be ecstatic about the video.

Finally, Leroy felt as if he was pulling his weight at SLH.

Without thinking, he reached into his shirt and gripped the chain around his neck.

See, Declan? I told you I would get out. I told you. I just hope you're proud of me, bro. Wherever you are, I hope you're proud.

Chapter 22

HANNA HURRIED BACK TO her car, but she didn't start it right away, deciding instead to sit behind the wheel and wait. As predicted, Dr. Fremont emerged from Sport Brain. She looked around before getting into a new BMW and then pulled out of the parking lot.

Hanna followed.

At first, she thought that Dr. Fremont was heading home—Jordyn, the secretary, had indicated that the doctor had no more patients for the day—or maybe to a boyfriend or girlfriend for an afternoon quickie. But when Dr. Fremont passed through upscale neighborhoods of the like that Hanna suspected someone of her status would live, it was clear that she had something else in mind.

Soon, the high-rises gave way to low-rises, which transitioned to more industrial, working class commercial enterprises: grungy buildings with gravel parking lots. The ubiquitous horns of coffee trucks melded with the sounds of machinery and filled the air.

Where are you going? Hanna wondered.

The answer soon became clear: Dr. Fremont pulled her BMW through a narrow opening in a chain-link fence and then got out.

Hanna couldn't see a sign anywhere but based on the car parts strewn haphazardly across the lot, it appeared to be either an auto mechanic or chop shop. Despite the fact that Dr. Fremont didn't fit in with either of these options, the woman didn't hesitate in walking toward the open garage door.

She'd been here before.

Hanna debated going after her, getting as close as possible, but decided against it. It wasn't that she was scared; not only was she capable of taking care of herself, but nothing that a greasy mechanic could do to her would compare to what she'd been through in the past.

Getting a metal chopstick through the chin was just the tip of the iceberg.

But dressed as she was, Hanna suspected that it would be near impossible to go unnoticed, and Dr. Fremont was already on to her.

Rather than getting out of the car, she pulled her cell phone out and wound down her window.

The video was grainy zoomed in like it was, but Hanna thought it still usable.

She started to record as the second a man in a blue polo stepped from the darkness and waddled up to Dr. Fremont.

"I know you," Hanna whispered, recognizing the man from Dr. Fremont's office.

As she watched, Dr. Fremont reached into her purse. Hanna's first thought was that she was going to remove a can of mace and douse the guy with it. But it wasn't mace she pulled out.

It was a wad of bills.

Hanna's bills.

"That's my money, you bitch."

Dr. Fremont pushed the cash against the guy's chest, but he didn't appear to want anything to do with it. When Dr. Fremont let go, however, the man caught the folded bills before they fell to the gravel.

Evidently satisfied, Dr. Fremont shouted something that Hanna couldn't make out, then turned to head back to her car.

Hanna sank down low in her seat but kept recording with her cell phone.

Looks like the good ol' doctor might not be so squeaky clean after all… looks like she might owe some shady characters a wee lil' bit of money, Hanna thought with a grin. *And if you want to get to the root cause of almost all bad things, all you have to do is follow the money.*

Chapter 23

"No, no idea where the gun is," Screech lied. He knew where the gun that had been used to kill Mark Magnusson was, of course; it was in the safe back at SLH Investigations where he'd put it.

What he didn't know, was where the gun *he'd* used to kill Captain Brandon Loomis was.

Detective Dunbar grunted, and Screech quickly changed the subject before the man asked any more questions.

"So, Shane Nolasco was killed right here, right in this ring with twenty-thousand people watching."

"Yeah. As you can see," Dunbar gestured to the canvas beneath their feet, "we took the mat that had been used during the fight to the lab for processing, and MSG has already replaced it with a new one. It's like nothing happened."

Except for the fact that Brock Page is still being held for questioning.

"Did you see the footage from the fight?"

"I did. Pretty gruesome stuff—I can't imagine what Shane's wife and daughter are going through right now. Personally, I've never been a fan of combat sports—I see enough violence every day in this job."

Screech nodded in agreement.

"Same. What about video cameras? They must have had a dozen or so recording during the fight... anything suspicious pop-up?"

"A dozen? Ha, talk about more like a hundred," Dunbar corrected. "Not only that, but MSG runs facial recognition software of every single person who steps into the building. Some of the most advanced software in the world. A tech from

MSG is helping organize the footage so that we can go through it all. Right now, it's a bit of a logistical nightmare."

"Any chance—"

"Nope," Dunbar said pre-emptively. "You can't see the footage."

Screech figured as much.

"So, what happens next?"

Dunbar turned his face to the rafters.

"Now we wait. The only reason I'm talking to you—other than the fact that I consider you a friend—is because so far Brock hasn't been charged with anything. We're still trying to track his movements after the fight. If he went to his manager's house, then we'll pass that along to the DA, see what he has to say about it."

Screech felt his chest start to tighten.

"What about Shane?"

"Well, that depends."

"On?"

"On whether or not the ME decides to record Shane's death as a homicide or not."

The tightness in Screech's chest started to make breathing difficult.

"The ME… it isn't… it isn't—"

Dunbar nodded.

"Oh, it is. The ME is our old friend, Dr. Beckett Campbell. He's performing the autopsy as we speak."

Chapter 24

AFTER PAYING OFF CHUBBY blue-shirt man, Dr. Fremont drove back to the city with Hanna once again following close behind. Something told her that the doctor's daily adventure wasn't quite done yet.

And when Dr. Fremont pulled her car up to the gated drive of an Estate in the Upper East Side, instead of pressing a button in her fancy car to open it, Hanna's suspicions were proven correct.

This wasn't the woman's house.

As Dr. Fremont walked over to the intercom and pressed the button, Hanna found herself in a similar situation as she'd been at the chop shop: crouched low, her cell phone recording through the open car window.

When no answer came, Dr. Fremont pressed the button once more and then started to pace. While she'd been angry handing over the money to the man in the blue shirt, she looked anxious now.

While biting the fingernails of one hand, Dr. Fremont started to mash the intercom button at increasingly shorter intervals.

Eventually, the door to the estate opened and a brunette came barreling out, desperately trying to cover herself with a silk robe as she walked. The robe didn't like being bossed around and did its best to reveal what was obviously a set of purchased breasts beneath.

Hanna didn't recognize the woman but could tell by the way she was gesturing that she was none too happy to see Dr. Fremont. Her face, on the other hand, held a neutral expression.

"Who the hell is this plastic surgery addict?" Hanna wondered out loud.

The woman tried to shoo Dr. Fremont away, but the latter was having none of it.

"Get out of here!" she shouted.

Dr. Fremont replied, but her voice was too low for Hanna to make out the words.

"This is your fault! It was your idea!"

Another inaudible reply.

This exchange continued for nearly a minute before the woman in the robe leaned forward and hissed something. Whatever she said caused Dr. Fremont to reel backward.

Then the doctor turned around and started back toward her car, tears filling her eyes.

"What in the—*shit!*"

Just as Dr. Fremont opened the door to her BMW, she saw Hanna.

"*Shit! Shit! Shit!*"

Hanna dropped her phone and started her car. Only, her car had already been running and when she turned the key a horrible grating sound filled the cab. She tried to put the VW into drive, but the lights on the dash lit up and then the car shut off.

"Hey! Hey you!" Dr. Fremont shouted, abandoning her own vehicle and starting across the road toward Hanna.

"No, c'mon, not now."

Hanna furiously tried to start the car again, but each time she turned the key the engine just clicked.

Dr. Fremont had something in her hand and was holding it out like a weapon.

A gun? Mace?

Hanna didn't even look; she focused her efforts on starting the car. But no matter how hard she pumped the brakes or how often she turned the key, it seemed to be clinically dead at this point.

Now she had a decision to make: roll up the window or keep trying to get the car moving.

The former might protect her from mace, but not from a bullet.

Hanna took her foot off the gas and pressed the brake, holding it down for a mental three count. In her periphery, she saw Dr. Fremont approaching the car, arm still outstretched. Whatever she intended on doing, the woman meant business.

Just as a hand snaked into her window, Hanna turned the key and the car finally burped to life.

"Yes!" she shouted, immediately knocking the stubborn vehicle into drive.

Hanna heard a hiss and a stream of liquid flew into the backseat. Then Dr. Fremont cried out as the window frame whacked against her wrist.

Hanna didn't stop; even as the bottle of mace quit rolling around the passenger seat, she just kept on driving.

Chapter 25

AFTER MEETING WITH JAMAAL, Leroy headed back to SLH investigation. Once there, he downloaded the video of Shane and Brock arguing onto the computer. Even though Screech was the one with a background in tech, Leroy spent most of his time in the computer lab in high school. In fact, if it weren't for SLH, he might've been heading to college to double major in chemistry and computer engineering. Still, despite his experience, and the help of sophisticated video editing software, Leroy could not, for the life of him, get rid of the damn skipping sound.

Rather than just giving up and waiting for Screech, he decided instead to play the video multiple times with the audio off and concentrate on reading lips.

Brock's lips, because Shane had his back to the camera.

After watching the video five or six times, Leroy came up with a script that seemed to work.

How can you be sure?

But did she tell you or are you just guessing?

I thought you said—unrecognizable—things were great for a while.

Maybe deal with it after the fight. After you get paid. You need to be fully—unrecognizable.

What? You can't be serious! Don't even fucking think about it.

After that last part, Brock reached out to shove Shane, but the man leaned back and then stormed out.

Oh, they were arguing alright. But about *what?*

Leroy stared at his chicken-scratch writing, trying to fill in the blanks, Shane's part of the conversation.

Money? Is Shane pissed about how much he's getting paid, which is probably less than Brock? Is she some sort of accountant? Was he going to back out of the fight? Is that what he shouldn't even think about?

This narrative almost worked, except for the mention of dealing with it after Shane got paid.

Instead of continuing to bash his head against a wall, Leroy searched the Internet to see just how much Shane and Brock got paid for their short bout.

What he found was surprising.

Brock made a whopping 2.5 million, while Shane only pulled in five-hundred grand. Not bad for one fight, but not the gaudy numbers he had been expecting.

Rumor had it that Floyd Mayweather had earned more than 300 million for his spectacle with Conor McGregor, with the Irishman pulling in a 100-million-dollar payday. Neither Shane nor Brock were close to that type of draw, of course, but Leroy had expected both men to be in the mid-seven figure range for this high-profile fight at MSG.

Sure, boxing had taken a backseat to MMA in terms of popularity, but betting was what drove boxer salaries more than anything.

With this in mind, Leroy started doing some research on the odds prior to the Page/Nolasco bout.

The opening line had Brock at a -240 favorite and Shane the underdog at +180. But these odds weren't static; the closer it got to the fight, the more the odds shifted in Brock's favor; the line closed at -400 and +275. This meant, at least to Leroy with his rudimentary knowledge of sports betting, that more people were putting money on Brock. To protect from massive losses, bookies—both legal and otherwise—compensated by lowering the payout for a Brock win.

But that wasn't the end of the story. In addition to picking an outright winner, there were dozens and dozens of prop bets, including what round the fight would end as well as the cause of the stoppage, and every possible permutation.

These odds were harder to research, but the closing odds on Brock winning by KO in the first round? -250.

"What the hell?"

The odds of a specific result in a specific round for Brock — the first round, no less — were actually greater than the opening line for Brock to win by *any* result. That was unheard of.

Leroy leaned away from the computer for a moment and then rubbed his eyes. The numbers didn't change.

Someone had put money on Brock knocking Shane out in the first. A *lot* of money.

"But who?" he asked out loud. "Who the hell knew that Shane was going down in the first? Who the hell knew that he was going to die in the ring?"

Chapter 26

OF COURSE IT WAS Beckett. He was, after all, the head ME for New York State. And a high-profile case such as this one — a boxer killed in the ring, a manager shot in his home — would draw the most experienced ME, regardless of how the man's colleagues felt about it.

But just the thought, the very idea of going to talk to Beckett again gave Screech heart palpitations.

Death… the man just reeked of death and it had nothing to do with his profession.

"In a couple of hours, after Dr. Campbell makes a decision on Shane's manner of death, we're either going to let Brock go or charge him. By then, I hope that we'll also have his boxing gloves and the gun in our possession."

The comment took Screech by surprise.

"Wait, whose gloves? *Brock's* gloves? You don't have Brock's gloves?"

Dunbar shook his head.

"No. Nobody knows what happened to them. We have video of his manager leaving after the fight and Brock exiting MSG shortly thereafter. Neither have the gloves on them, and they aren't in any of the dressing rooms."

"Did Brock have anything with him when he left?"

"His gym bag but judging by the size it's doubtful that the gloves were in there."

Dunbar fell silent and the expression on his face suggested that he felt uncomfortable sharing any more. Even though Screech was grateful for what he'd already learned — he hadn't even expected to get inside MSG — he decided to push a little harder.

"What are the chances you can hold off on making a decision about Brock if things don't come back in his favor? Could you give me a little time… a couple of days, maybe? I doubt I have to tell you this, but things have been… difficult… without Drake in the picture."

Dunbar rocked his head from side-to-side.

"I wish I could help, Screech—I really do. But the DA… between you and me? There are rumors that he's going to throw his hat in the ring—pardon the pun—for mayor. The longer this thing remains in limbo the worse it looks for him."

"The DA? Mark Trumbo?"

"That's him."

Screech closed his eyes and massaged his temples. He hadn't slept long the night prior, and the few hours he'd gotten had been interrupted. The gun that he'd used to shoot Captain Loomis was missing, Sergeant Yasiv was up for murder, and things didn't look good for Brock. There was also the Nick Petrazzino situation, and the fact that they still had no idea what happened to the USB key that they were supposed to steal from DA Trumbo.

"What a mess," he whispered.

"Tell me about it."

Screech opened his eyes and looked at Detective Dunbar.

"Well," he said, in a tired voice, "thanks for letting me in here. I really appreciate it. I'm going to do everything I can for my client, but if I find out anything that convinces me that Brock is guilty? I'm coming to you with it. That's a promise."

Dunbar's brow knitted, then relaxed.

"Sounds good to me. I'm guessing that you're off to visit our mutual friend?"

It took Screech a moment to figure out who the man was referring to, but Dunbar didn't give him a chance to answer.

"Yeah, I can see it in your eyes. A little piece of advice, Screech?"

"What's that?"

"Dr. Beckett Campbell… I know he's your friend, but perhaps it's best not to get too close to the man."

Now it was Screech's turn to stare. He wasn't sure exactly what Dunbar was alluding to, how much the detective really knew about Beckett, but it was clear that he knew *something*.

Enough to give Screech a warning.

"Sage advice," Screech replied, extending his hand. "Thanks for letting me in here and giving me the head's up. If you need anything from me in the future, you know where to find me. So long as we can pay the electrical bills, that is."

Chapter 27

BEFORE HEADING TO NYU Med, Screech sent out a text to Hanna and Leroy. Neither replied, which was slightly disconcerting, so he sent a follow-up message telling them to meet back at the office in about an hour or so.

He hoped that they weren't responding because they were making more progress than he was. In his estimation, as it stood now, if Brock was charged with murder, his prospects didn't look good.

Screech was also stalling. The last time he'd seen Beckett, the man had told him in no uncertain terms that their relationship was effectively terminated. And that was before all the mysterious deaths that Screech had uncovered.

For about the hundredth time since Drake had left for Columbia, Screech wished that he was here. Screech had become more confident in his abilities, and his decision-making, but Drake was the one behind SLH, irrespective of the names on the door. He was the PI, he was the ex-detective, and he would know how to deal with complicated situations such as this one.

But Drake wasn't here, and he was probably never coming back.

After spending a few more minutes collecting himself, Screech hurried across the parking lot and then made his way inside the building. From there, he took the familiar, if winding route through the sterile halls until he reached the Pathology Department. He hoped to run into Beckett along the way so that he wouldn't have to deal with the curmudgeonly secretary who'd stonewalled him last time, but he had no such luck.

"Hi," he said with a smile.

The woman's upper lip curled a little.

"How can I help you?"

Screech looked around, trying to catch a glimpse of either Beckett or Susan, but neither were visible.

"I'm looking for Beckett," he said. It took considerable effort to keep the phony smile on his face while he spoke.

To his surprise, the secretary smiled back.

"Your name is Screech, isn't it?" she asked.

Screech debated offering a pseudonym but didn't bother. He'd lied enough for one day.

"Yep, that's me. Is Beckett here?"

The secretary shook her head, but her smile didn't falter.

"No, he's down in the morgue, but you can go see him if you want."

Screech gaped.

What the hell is going on here?

The experience with this woman was so different than before that it was almost comical. Screech had to resist the urge to glance in either direction, to confirm that this was indeed the Pathology Department and not some sort of movie set.

"Uh, I, uh, I—I can?"

The woman laughed; she actually laughed. The secretary who had told him with a straight face that Beckett wasn't in his office even though Screech could see him hiding beneath his desk, seemed almost giddy.

And it was infectious. If today were any other day, Screech might have chuckled along with her.

But not today. Not after losing the gun, after Shane died in the ring.

"Okay, thanks," he said hesitantly. "Is he… expecting me?"

The woman's smile grew until it filled her entire, wide face.

"Of course, Beckett always has time for his friends."

Chapter 28

DR. BECKETT CAMPBELL WHISTLED as he worked. He knew it was clichéd and he knew that it was also frowned upon by the medical community as a whole. After all, doctors were supposed to be serious and unfeeling automatons strictly focused on medicine and science.

But he didn't give a shit what other people thought. Never had, and hopefully never would.

Beckett pulled the sheet off the first body and examined the cadaver superficially, first looking at the man's head and then his nude body with the same level of attention as a potential suitor on Grindr. Or so he'd heard.

Usually, he performed this ritual before looking at any of the accompanying paperwork or listening to cop theories in order to avoid bias. In this case, however, foreknowledge was unavoidable.

Still, even Beckett was beholden to some rituals, and this was one of them.

The man on the metal gurney was young, likely in his mid-thirties. He had a shaved head and wide-set eyes that were encircled with pre-mortem bruising. His nose was out of true, an indication of a previous break. The most alarming feature, however, was the dent smack in the center of his forehead.

Beckett made a mental note of this, then inspected the man's body.

Shane Nolasco was in excellent shape, with well-defined muscles and proportionality. His skin appeared a little thin, but Beckett attributed this to pre-fight weight cutting and subsequent minor dehydration. The man's hands were large and the knuckles thick, likely from previous breaks.

Satisfied, Beckett returned to the man's face. He used gloved fingers to open Shane's eyelids and stared down at the bloodshot eyes beneath. Then he palpated the man's forehead, gently pressing the circumference of the indentation.

The skull had far too much give to it.

Ah, there's the problem.

Made mostly of cortical bone, the top of the forehead was one of the strongest bones in the body. That, combined with its impact resistant shape, made forehead skull fractures — especially ones of this magnitude — exceedingly rare.

Beckett's eyes darted over at the sheet of paper affixed to the clipboard on a small side table. He knew that he should be filling out information about the cadaver, but he was just too damn excited to see what secrets Shane's brain was hiding.

"After, after," he promised himself. Then, with a grin on his face, he reached for a scalpel.

To gain access to the skull, the scalp first needed to be removed. To this end, Beckett pressed the scalpel to the area near Shane's temple where his ear met the side of his face, then made a long incision up over the top of his head to an identical spot on the other side.

Shane not having any hair saved a few steps and meant that Beckett wouldn't be spitting it out for an hour or two after the autopsy.

New rule: everyone must shave their heads before they die.

He was just starting to peel the skin down over the forehead, dissecting the pericranium as he went, when the elevator pinged.

Beckett looked up, expecting to see the mousy Dr. Karen Nordmeyer strutting out, but it wasn't her.

"Screech?" He was so surprised that the scalpel nearly slipped from his hand. "What the hell are you doing here?"

Chapter 29

THERE WAS SOMETHING DIFFERENT about Dr. Campbell, something that Screech picked up on even before he approached: a lightness, a levity that he couldn't remember seeing in the ME before now.

"Well, I, uhh, I'm just here to…" Screech let his sentence trail off.

What he was here for was to pry information about Shane Nolasco's death before it was shared with the cops or the press. *That* was what he was here to do.

"Yeah, okay, it doesn't really matter," Dr. Campbell said dismissively. He indicated a clipboard with a wave of his hand. "Because I'm looking for another set of hands."

"Excuse me?"

"Bro, I need some help and the other ME is a raging cunt. Grab the clipboard and use your hands for something other than smothering your micropenis."

More confused than he'd been with the secretary upstairs, Screech's legs seemed to have a life of their own and carried him toward the small table. There, he picked up the clipboard and stared at it as if it contained advanced calculus instead of a simple checklist. Shane Nolasco's name was at the top along with his date of birth. Next came a list of physical characteristics.

"What's this?" he asked.

"Work—the good stuff," Beckett said, stepping off to one side.

And that's when Screech saw him. He was no stranger to dead bodies, and even though he'd prepared himself for the eventuality of seeing Shane Nolasco's corpse, he didn't expect it to be so raw, so visceral.

So real.

Shane was lying on his back, naked, his hands at his sides, the palms up. This alone was disturbing, but the red line that ran over the top of his head made Screech's stomach lurch.

He looked away and Beckett chuckled.

"Okay, fine, I'll do the hard part. I'll shout out some random nonsense, you write it down.

"Okay," Screech agreed, his eyes locked on the checklist.

"Good—already you're smarter than half of the MEs in this joint. We'll start with the easy stuff: male, brown eyes, shaved head."

Screech scribbled down the information as it was delivered to him.

"5'11, approximately 177 pounds."

Beckett moved down the body, describing a myriad of injuries as he went. Screech suddenly found himself struggling to keep up, but he was game. Beckett was right, this was just administrative bullshit.

When the doctor took a break to inspect Shane's fingernails, Screech decided that now was the time to speak up.

"You hear about Sergeant Yasiv?" Screech stared at Dr. Campbell as he spoke, trying to see if there was any change in his demeanor, his posture, anything.

Beckett gave nothing away.

"Sure, I heard. It's a shame, too, because he really was a nice guy."

A fairly benign comment, but Screech detected a hint of defensiveness buried beneath.

"He didn't do it," Screech blurted.

This time, Beckett stopped what he was doing and turned to face Screech.

"Really? You sure? I mean, he went to South Carolina… I have complete faith in our boys in blue. They would never lie, cheat, deal drugs, kill innocent people, you get my drift."

As he spoke, Beckett started to work his way down Shane's abdomen and toward his groin.

"South Carolina?"

Beckett used two fingers to flip the man's penis up onto his belly like a limp noodle. Screech cringed, and he felt butterflies in his stomach, but he found himself unable to look away.

"Yeah, that narcissistic reverend and his holy wife." When Screech still didn't answer, Beckett added, "You know, the people he is accused of murdering?"

Beckett stared at Screech as he fondled the man's testicles.

Screech gagged and looked away.

"No, I meant—I meant Captain Loomis."

"Yeah, but what about Captain Loomis?"

Beckett cupped the man's balls and gave them an affectionate squeeze.

"Ah, you mean the big bastard who was shot outside the Loomis estate? That Captain Loomis?"

Screech nodded, but he suddenly wanted to change the subject. He wasn't even sure why he'd brought it up in the first place.

I should have listened to Hanna. I should have never mentioned Captain Loomis.

"Yasiv's being charged with that, too? Huh. Well, yeah, of course, he didn't do that—we *both* know he didn't do that."

There was a lot to unpack in that statement, but Beckett flopped Shane's penis back over his balls and quickly moved on.

"Minor testicular atrophy, likely due to exogenous testosterone administration."

Screech's mind was racing.

"Screech, jot it down, brother."

He found a line for 'Additional Information' and wrote: *testicular atrophy.*

What did Beckett mean by that? We both know Yasiv didn't do that… how could Beckett be so sure? Does he know I shot him?

Screech shook his head.

No. Impossible. Only Hanna and I know.

But that was a lie; there was someone with Hanna that night, someone who had helped her escape from the basement.

"What's wrong with you, Screech? Never seen a man's balls before? Well, get over it. Now it's time for the good stuff. That funk, that sweet, that nasty stuff."

Beckett made his way to the head of the table and slipped his fingers into the incision that ran across Shane's scalp. There was a horrible sucking sound as Beckett started to peel back the man's skin.

Screech gagged again, and bile burned the back of his throat.

"You see that, there at the bottom of the page?"

Screech focused on the page, his eyes watering.

"Yeah," he said in a hoarse whisper.

"Good. Under cause of death, write blunt force trauma to the skull."

Screech did as he was asked, and then his eyes fell on the last line: *Manner of Death.*

This, Screech knew, was the most important thing on the checklist. The manner of death would determine if Brock was released or charged with murder.

He tapped the pen several times in anticipation, but when Beckett didn't tell him what to write, he finally conjured the courage to look up.

"What about the manner of—"

He stopped speaking when he realized that Beckett was on his cell phone. Noticing Screech's stare, Beckett put the phone on speaker and placed it on the gurney beside Shane's corpse.

It rang twice, and a male voice answered.

"Hello?"

"Hey Doogie, it's Beckett."

"Good afternoon, Dr. Campbell."

Beckett reached out and covered the phone with his palm.

"It's my Savant assistant," he told Screech with a grin.

"I'm not your assistant, Dr. Campbell, I'm your resident."

The muscles in Beckett's face tightened, but the smile remained.

"Yes, of course. And what a resident you are. Listen, Grant, I've got a question for you."

"Sure, go ahead."

"How much force would it take to fracture the frontal bone?"

"Of a human being?"

"No, a fucking dolphin—of course, a human being. I'm talking massive fracture that spiderwebs to the supraorbital processes."

"Well, that depends on the age of the person, as well as the gender and—"

Beckett rolled his eyes.

"Thirty-ish-year-old male, white."

"There are many factors involved, most important being the size and shape of the object, but I'll go out on a limb and say over a thousand-foot-pounds of force."

Beckett made a face if to see say, *I told you he was my Savant assistant.*

"Great. And what's the average force of a punch from a professional fighter?"

"With eight or twelve-ounce gloves?"

"I dunno, the big goofy red ones."

"Twelve ounces. On average, a professional boxer will deliver seven hundred and seventy-six-foot-pounds of force per punch."

"And what's the hardest ever punch recorded?" Beckett asked.

Screech didn't know if the man on the other end of the line, this Grant or Doogie or whatever his name was, was reading something off the Internet or if he was producing it from memory. Either way, the lack of lag time between the question and answer was impressive.

"Controversial; but I'd go with Frank Bruno at nine-hundred and twenty-foot pounds of force."

"All right, I owe you one, sweetheart. Keep it right, keep it tight."

Beckett hung up the phone and then glanced at Shane's rumpled scalp that had been pulled down over his eyes.

Then he looked up and stared directly at Screech.

"The manner of death is homicide, Screech. Make sure you write that down in big, bold letters. Homicide… with a capital *H.*"

PART III

Mens Rea

Chapter 30

WHEN SCREECH MADE IT back to SLH investigations, he was surprised to find both Leroy and Hanna waiting for him.

"You guys don't know how to text? Don't—"

Hanna hushed him and pointed at the TV mounted on the wall. With a frown, Screech silently slid beside them and watched as District Attorney Mark Trumbo approached the pedestal and adjusted the mic.

"Good evening and thank you for joining us," the DA began. Even though he was a much different man than Ken Smith, he was larger and more bombastic, yet less refined, there were elements about him that reminded Screech of the former mayor. "First off, I would like to offer my sincerest condolences to the Nolasco family, to his wife Nadine, and to his daughter Andrea. Last night, tragedy befell not just Shane Nolasco in the ring, but also Mark Magnusson, a long-time boxing promoter and manager, who was shot and killed in his home. The ME has classified both cases as homicides, and we believe that they are connected. My team and I, including the NYPD, worked tirelessly through the night to piece together exactly what happened, both in Madison Square Garden and in Mark Magnusson's home. And this morning, the ME classified both deaths as homicides. I am here before you today to announce that we have indicted Brock Page for both of their murders."

The DA paused as any good showman would and the crowd broke into chatter. He silenced them with his hands.

"Brock has turned himself in without incident and has been cooperative. As the details of this case are still unfolding and it is considered active, I am limited in what I can tell you at this time. That being said, I will now open the floor to questions."

The crowd chatter intensified but died down when the DA extended a finger at a diminutive man with a notepad.

"DA Trumbo, you said that the ME considers Shane Nolasco's death as a homicide. Is this specific to the circumstances surrounding Shane's death, or would any death inside the ring be considered a homicide?"

"The ME considers all factors before assigning manner of death, Bill. Where and how the victim died is only part of the investigative process."

"But it was clear from fight footage that Shane died from blows to the head. Did your team uncover any aggravating circumstances? Are there any camera angles that the press and public currently don't have access to?"

The DA shook his head.

"At this time, I'm unable to get into specifics about Shane's death. All I can say is that the ME considers it a homicide, and we at the DA's office concur. Next."

Trumbo signaled a woman with short blonde hair tucked behind her ears.

"Can you tell us more about how Mark Magnusson died and how these two cases are related?"

The DA seemed to mull this over for a moment before answering.

"Mark Magnusson was killed by a single gunshot wound to the head. We believe that these murders are connected due to the relationships between the victims and Brock Page as well as the time frame in which they were committed."

"What about motive? Do we have a motive for these murders?" someone blurted.

"At this time, specifics related to motive are under investigation. But I will remind you that a motive is not necessary to file an indictment for any crime, irrespective of the severity."

"What about the murder weapon? Was the gun used to kill Mark Magnusson found at the scene? On Brock's person?"

"That's another detail that I am unable to discuss at this time." DA Trumbo's lips became a thin line as he leaned away from the pedestal. "That's enough questions for now; I will update you periodically as the case moves forward. Thank you for your patience."

With that, the man walked toward the building behind him, with his aides, people who Screech recognized from their recon, following close behind. The camera zoomed out and talking heads filled the screen.

Leroy, who had the remote, muted the television.

"Well, looks like our timeframe just got shorter," Hanna said in an airy tone.

Screech nodded.

Dunbar had told him that the DA was going to push hard on this one, but even Screech had thought they'd get at least a full twenty-four hours before Brock was charged.

They had to work faster, had to unearth something that would exonerate Brock before the weekend was up.

"Monday morning," he said absently. When Hanna and Screech looked at him, he clarified. "Brock is going to go before a judge Monday morning for his arraignment and when that footage airs, it won't matter the outcome of a trial. The man will be as good as guilty in the eyes of the public."

"Yeah, but I still don't understand," Leroy said, shaking his head. Screech noticed that there was bruising on his chin and that he was slightly tilted to one side as if protecting his ribs. "How can Shane's death be a homicide? I mean, obviously Mark's death was murder, but Shane's? Brock couldn't have *intended* to kill his friend, could he?"

Screech cleared his throat.

"I think we should sit down—I just came back from the ME's office, from the morgue. It gets worse. This entire fucking case is worse than we thought."

Chapter 31

"I SAW SHANE'S BODY... there's no way that what happened to him was normal. The man's skull was completely caved in. According to the ME, this kind of damage simply can't happen in a normal boxing match using normal gloves."

"Wait—the gloves were modified somehow?"

Screech shrugged.

"No one knows where they are, so it's just speculation for now."

Leroy made a face.

"What? Normally the commission takes the gloves after the fight. Given that they're evidence, I'm sure that the NYPD would have confiscated them."

"Then you'd be wrong; I spoke to Detective Dunbar and the NYPD doesn't have them. Apparently, in the chaos following Shane's collapse, they went missing. Which means that we need to find those gloves before anyone else does."

Leroy nodded, then absently rubbed his jaw.

"What the hell happened to you, by the way?"

Leroy cocked his head to one side.

"It's a long story. But let's just say my visit to Pike's gym was, well, painful, to say the least."

"Was it worth it?"

Leroy shrugged.

"Maybe, not sure yet. I did manage to get a video that is very interesting. Here, let me show you."

They gathered around Leroy's computer and watched the video several times while Leroy read his notes.

"I'm thinking they were fighting about money, 'cuz—"

Hanna cut Leroy off.

"No, not money—that's about a woman," she said matter-of-factly. "They're arguing about a woman. I'd say that Shane was pissed because someone is sleeping with his wife."

Hanna's confidence surprised Screech.

"Really? You sure?"

She frowned.

"Trust me, I know jealousy when I see it."

He pictured Hanna's ex-husband as the man tore through their office.

Yeah, I suppose you do, he thought.

"Okay, okay, what about you, Hanna? How did your visit to the psychiatrist go?"

"Well, I too have some videos to show you—I'm thinking that Dr. Fremont has some financial problems and is looking for an easy fix."

After watching the two videos, one taken outside of what looked like a scrap yard and the other a fancy upscale mansion, Screech concurred with his partner's assessment.

"Can you—can you, uh, play the video where she goes to the house again?" Leroy asked tentatively.

Hanna nodded and replayed the video of Dr. Fremont outside the estate. When the woman in the silk robe came out, he told her to pause it.

"You looking for a nip slip, Leroy?" Hanna asked.

Leroy ignored her and tapped the screen.

"Can you zoom in on her face."

Screech took the helm and managed to blow the image up.

"I think I know who that is," Leroy whispered. But instead of elucidating, he grabbed the mouse from Screech's hand and opened the browser. A second later, there were two images on the screen, side-by-side.

"Shit, you know what? I think you're right," Screech said. "That's Shane Nolasco's wife. Now, why the hell would Brock's psychiatrist pay a visit to Shane's wife?"

***

"So, we've got a shady psychiatrist who visits the wife of the deceased, even though she's treating Brock, and she also takes your money and gives it to a repo man of sorts," Screech said, laying out the facts as plainly as he could.

"Yeah, speaking about the money? I didn't get a receipt, but I'll need to be reimbursed," Hanna said, but Screech ignored her.

If they didn't solve this case, Hanna getting her five-hundred bucks back would be the least of their worries.

"We also have video of an argument between Shane and Brock a week before their match, likely related to a woman. And Brock's gloves from the fight are missing."

A silence fell over the trio. Leroy and Hanna had done some good work, but all they really had was evidence of a series of strange, yet seemingly unconnected events.

Certainly not enough for DA Trumbo to rethink the indictment.

"What about Mark Magnusson's death? Should we focus on that at all?" Leroy asked.

It was a valid question, but Screech didn't think so.

"The DA might have the wrong man in cuffs, but he's right about one thing: the two cases are related. We need to keep focusing on Shane's death; we find out what really happened to him, and Mark's will also fall into place."

"Focus on Shane's death…" Leroy mused. "So, like, what do we do now?"

Drake would know what to do, Screech thought. Unfortunately, he didn't and said as much.

"Well, in that case, we need to go back to MSG. Or at least get access to the footage from before and after the fight," Hanna suggested.

"That's gonna be tough," Screech replied.

"Why? Can't you talk to your buddy in the NYPD again? Dunbar?"

Screech summarized his conversation with the Detective to Leroy and Hanna.

"I don't see the problem," Hanna said when he was finished.

"Maybe you weren't listening, Hanna, but Dunbar pretty much said that if Shane's death is considered a homicide, he won't be able to share anything with me—or us."

"I don't see it that way."

Screech was too tired for games and pinched the bridge of his nose.

"Fuck, Hanna, why don't—"

"The way I see it? The man is looking to make a trade."

"A trade?"

Now it was Hanna's turn to look annoyed.

"Yeah, a trade. But the real question we should be asking ourselves is whether we believe Brock… whether we think he really is innocent."

A lightbulb went off in Screech's head as he finally clued into what the woman was talking about.

"Shit, you know what? I think you're right. But here's the thing, it really doesn't matter if we think he's innocent or not. I warned Brock, I warned him that if he was guilty, I'd go to the DA myself. I *warned* him."

"Umm, guys?" Leroy asked, looking confused as ever. "You want to tell me what you're talking about?"

"The gun," Hanna said flatly. "Dunbar needs Mark's murder weapon and we need footage from MSG. I bet he'd be open to a trade."

Leroy frowned.

"But if Brock is guilty, giving up the gun pretty much seals his fate," he said. "Which will be twenty-five to life, heavy on the life part."

Chapter 32

"WELL, I DON'T SEE what choice we have. It's our only bargaining chip and if we don't get a look at what really happened at MSG, Brock is going to prison anyway," Screech said, verbalizing what they were all thinking.

"So that settles it, then. While you do that, I'll continue to work the Dr. Fremont angle, try to find out why the hell she was visiting Nadine Nolasco," Hanna offered.

Screech squinted at her. Even though she hadn't come right out and said it, it was obvious that her whole Russian tennis star gig hadn't worked out as planned.

"Hanna, we gotta keep this all above board. If we do anything illegal..."

"Oh, so now *I'm* the one who's being stereotyped, is that it? Now, I know how you feel, Leroy."

Leroy rolled his eyes.

"Don't worry, Screech, I'll keep your name out of the press when they arrest me," she mocked.

"Hanna..."

"I'm kidding, I get it. Everything above board."

Screech remained unconvinced. It still amazed him that Hanna hadn't gone to prison for helping Drake escape the psychiatric unit. But that had only been because of Sergeant Yasiv's influence. Screech had a sneaking suspicion that the man didn't have the same sort of clout as he used to.

But he bit his tongue. She was a grown woman, one who didn't take kindly to being told what to do.

"What about me?" Leroy chimed in.

Screech observed the man's bruised chin.

"You should probably just rest up. If your mom —"

Before he could finish the sentence, there was a heavy knock at the door.

Screech's eyes went wide, and he glanced at Hanna, who had immediately gone to her desk to retrieve her gun.

He looked to Leroy next and stopped the man in his tracks.

"The office," he hissed.

Leroy shook his head and Screech looked desperately at the shadowy figure behind the frosted glass.

"Leroy, get in the office!"

But the man was obstinate; instead of hiding away in the office like Screech wanted, he went to his computer instead.

"What the hell are you doing?" He was trying to keep his voice down, but it kept rising.

With every subsequent knock, Screech could feel his blood pounding in his temples.

It's Jimmy… he's back to finish the job.

Gritting his teeth, he looked to Hanna for support. But she seemed unusually calm given the circumstances.

Probably because she's holding a gun in her hand, the gun she's going to use to kill her ex-husband if you don't do something first.

"Leroy, get in the—"

The man pulled back from his computer.

"It's not Jimmy," he informed them.

"Just get the fuck in the—"

"It's not Jimmy," Leroy repeated, indicating his computer monitor. "I installed a camera above the door."

Screech was supposed to do that, but he'd forgotten. Just like he'd forgotten to get rid of the gun used to kill Loomis.

What the hell is wrong with me?

"Who is it then?" Hanna demanded.

"It's not Jimmy, but it might as well be… this guy doesn't look happy at all. Like, *at all*."

Chapter 33

NICK PETRAZZINO WAS SIX-foot-three, closer to three hundred than two hundred pounds, with a square jaw and short black hair. Sporting a navy suit and white shirt without a tie, he looked like a banker or real estate agent.

But Screech knew better. While he wasn't sure what the man's legitimate business enterprises were, he wouldn't be surprised if waste management made up a significant portion of his portfolio.

"I'm a little disappointed with you guys if I'm being honest," Nick said as he took a seat in Screech's chair. He eyed the cracked screen curiously but didn't mention it. "As I said from our previous meeting, the two things I don't care for are leaving my restaurant and dishonest people."

Screech swallowed hard and looked over at Hanna. While she was no longer holding her gun, it was on her desk, within plain sight and arm's reach.

"And I'm hoping that today I am subjected to only one of those things. You told me that you could get the USB from the DA, but based on what I saw on TV, it appears as if his security detail has become more robust."

The DA doesn't have the USB key anymore, Screech almost said. *And we have no idea who does.*

"I'm sorry about the delay, Mr. Petrazzino," Screech began, trying to keep his voice as even as possible. "Your case is a priority for us at SLH, but we have another time sensitive matter that we are attending to. That being said, we *will* retrieve the USB key."

Nick leaned forward, and the chair creaked under his weight. It was clear that while he was unabashedly polite, this man was not somebody you wanted to make enemies of.

Or owe favors to.

"Oh, I know you will. But I'm a reasonable man, and I understand that these things take time."

Benign words, spoken without inflection, but for some reason, Screech detected a hint of a threat in them.

"Yes, of course. We will get the USB key."

Nick held his stare for a second longer than comfortable and then leaned back again.

"Good. Now, what's this other, time-sensitive case that's been bogging you down?"

"It's a high-profile client, but we can't discuss—"

Nick waved his hand, silencing Screech. Then he turned around to face Leroy, whose eyes were as big as silver dollars.

"What's this case, Leroy?"

Leroy glanced at Screech and then shrugged.

"I don't think—"

Once again, Nick silenced Screech, this time with a raised finger.

If it had been anyone else disrespecting him like this in his castle, Screech wouldn't have stood for it.

But this wasn't just anybody. This was Nick Fucking Petrazzino.

Accepting Nick's case had been a desperate move, one that Screech instantly regretted. But SLH was sinking and the man had arrived with a life raft at just the right moment.

A fucking mistake...

Screech made a promise to himself that once they got the man his USB key they were going to sever all ties with him. And then, moving forward, he'd use just a modicum of discretion when it came to accepting new clients.

If we get the USB... but we have to find it first.

Screech nodded to Leroy.

"Brock Page," he answered dryly.

Nick's thick dark eyebrows traveled up his forehead.

"Really? Well, that's interesting. In the interest of getting my own case resolved, is there any way that I might be of assistance?"

Screech would've blurted no, had Nick's finger not remained raised.

Leroy looked at Screech again, then lowered his gaze.

Don't do it, Leroy. Please.

"Actually, there might be something that you can help us with."

"And what migh: that be?" Nick said, a hint of a smile forming on his lips.

"The betting lines," Leroy continued, gaining confidence. "I think… I think that somebody put a chunk of change on Brock winning by KO in the first round, not long before the fight."

Nick's smile vanished.

"Why would you think that I know anything about that? I run a food and beverage company, as well as a restaurant."

Leroy's confidence sluiced off him like ice on a warming windshield.

"Leroy just thought—"

Nick whipped his head around and glared at Screech.

"I asked Leroy, and Leroy will answer," he said sternly.

Behind the big man, Screech saw Hanna twitch, and for one horrible second, he thought she was going to reach for the gun.

If she did, that wouldn't just be the end of SLH Investigations, it would be the end of their lives, as well.

Hanna resisted the urge, and they both watched in horror as Nick returned his eyes to Leroy.

"I don't… I'm not… I just…"

Sweat broke out on his forehead.

"That's okay, Leroy. You know what? I like you, and I need that USB. If helping you can free up some of your time, I'll make a call or two."

Nick grabbed a sheet of paper off Screech's desk and scrawled a phone number on it.

"In case you need any other favors," he said, rising to his feet. Then to Screech, he added, "The next time I have to leave my restaurant, I'll expect it's because you have a package for me. Am I clear?"

"Crystal." Screech's throat was so constricted that he could barely speak. "Crystal clear, Mr. Petrazzino."

Chapter 34

"WHAT THE HELL WERE you thinking?" Screech nearly shouted as soon as Nick Petrazzino left their building. "Leroy, what the hell were you thinking?"

Leroy looked more frightened now than in Nick's presence.

"Screech, he's just—"

Screech shook Hanna off of him and took an aggressive step toward Leroy.

"You know who that is? You know who Nick Petrazzino is, right?"

Leroy looked downward as he wiped the sweat from his brow.

"What was he supposed to do?" Hanna implored.

"Anything but ask the man for a goddamn favor. Christ, have you ever seen the Godfather?"

Leroy raised his eyes, but the fear was gone.

It had been replaced with anger.

"What the fuck, Screech? You're the one who brought him in here. You're the one who agreed to take his case. Don't put this all on me."

Screech aimed a finger at the center of his own chest.

"What choice did I have? I'm doing everything I can to keep that door open. While you two," he took his finger and wagged it back and forth between Hanna and Leroy, "you two keep trying to fuck that up."

As soon as the words had come out of his mouth, Screech regretted them.

"You're doing this again?" Hanna said, her brow furrowing. "This fucking, I'm responsible for you guys, bullshit? Well, if you're going to play that game, Leroy's right: you brought that mobster in here, you accepted the job. So, what, Leroy's supposed to just keep mum when the man offers to help? That's what you wanted him to do?"

The retort that came to Screech's lips was something along the lines that she wasn't squeaky clean, that she'd drawn her psycho ex-husband here and he was arguably more dangerous than Nick Petrazzino.

But he stopped the words a split-second before they were spoken; after all, the gun was still close enough for Hanna to grab.

"Fuck," he blurted. "Guys, I'm—"

"No, don't do that; don't apologize, because it doesn't get you off the hook. Instead, you take that goddamn gun and go talk to Dunbar. Once we get Brock out of prison, we'll deal with Nick Petrazzino. You keep acting like it's you who has everything to lose, Screech, but we all do. We're all in deep here."

Hanna was brash, crude, and loyal to a fault.

More often than not, she was right, as well.

But not this time.

Hanna was wrong about how much they all had to lose. Sure, Leroy had given up the chance to go to college, but he was young and still had time to make changes, should it come to that. As for Hanna, her getting Drake out of the psychiatric institute and Dr. Kruk escaping in the process was behind her.

Sergeant Yasiv had seen to that.

But if it ever came to light what Screech had done, that he'd murdered Captain Loomis, he'd spend the rest of his life behind bars.

That's what he had to lose.

Maybe I can be Brock's cellmate, he thought incoherently.

"The gun," he said, staring at his two partners.

"Yeah, the gun," Hanna repeated, pointing towards the office door. "Go get the gun out of the safe and go talk to Dunbar."

Screech nodded, but Hanna had misinterpreted which gun he was referring to.

The gun he'd put in the safe was important because it would either condemn Brock Page or set him free.

But there was another gun out there somewhere, a gun that can only do one thing: put Screech behind bars for a long, long time.

Chapter 35

HANNA HAD PROMISED SCREECH that she wouldn't do anything illegal, but that had been a lie. The reality was that while Screech and Leroy had their particular set of skills, Hanna had hers.

And often times hers transcended the law.

Which is why she found herself outside Sport Brain once more, only this time she wasn't wearing a ridiculous tennis outfit but all black with a hood pulled over her head. And instead of sporting an imitation Coach purse, she carried a small case of lock-picking tools.

The real estate office and insurance company that flanked Sport Brain had since closed and the parking lot was empty, save a sole Mercedes.

Dr. Fremont, it appeared, had not returned after her encounter with Nadine Nolasco.

Hanna waited patiently until the front of Sport Brain opened and the blonde secretary came out. The woman locked the door behind her and then got into the Mercedes and drove off.

To be safe, Hanna sat in her car for another five minutes, just to be certain that the ditzy blonde hadn't forgotten anything and decided to come back. Eventually satisfied that there was a low likelihood of being interrupted, she slowly made her way across the street.

On her first visit, Hanna had noted a security camera stationed outside the insurance firm, but none by the real estate office or Sport Brain. She was careful to approach Dr. Fremont's office from the right, making sure to keep her hooded head low just in case the camera was equipped with a wide-angle lens.

It took less than a minute to pick the lock on the front door and then, without raising her head to look around—a common mistake criminals made and a hard habit to break—Hanna stepped inside.

Without hesitating, she went straight to Dr. Fremont's office, passing the secretary's desk without even looking at it.

Hanna was prepared to pick this lock too, but there was no need: Dr. Fremont had forgotten to lock it.

"Not so smart, after all," she whispered with a grin.

Hanna knew that time was of the essence, but when her eyes fell on the woman's chair tucked neatly beneath her desk, the urge was too great to ignore.

She sat in it, put her feet up and then did her best Dr. Fremont impression.

"I follow the WTA and I know you're not a tennis star. I just know it. I know *eeeeverything*."

With a chuckle, she swiveled around and stared at the wall of cabinets. There were no names on the outside, but she knew that they were alphabetized.

Dr. Fremont would have it no other way.

Starting from the top, she counted to ten across, then six on the second row. Hopping out of the seat, Hanna quickly inspected the lock. It was so pedestrian that she didn't even need her tools. Instead, she took a letter opener off the desk and pushed it into the slot.

It turned with only a little pressure.

"This is almost too easy."

The 'P' cabinet held folders belonging to five different patients, but by far the largest one was labeled *Page, Brock.*

Smiling now, she grabbed the hefty folder and returned to Dr. Fremont's desk.

Then she leaned back in the chair and started to read.

Chapter 36

SCREECH WAS SITTING IN his car outside 62nd precinct, staring absently at a handful of officers who were idly chatting, when there was a knock on the passenger window.

He sat bolt upright and gestured for Dunbar to open the car door. The man obliged but didn't get in.

"I got your message, Screech," Dunbar said, his face hard. "But I'm not sure that you got mine. Brock Page has been indicted for two homicides, and I know you and your PI firm are representing him. I can't talk to you."

Screech glanced around nervously. There was always the possibility that, despite their history, Dunbar would just take the gun from him and throw him in jail for obstruction.

Roger Schneiderman had told him that this was unlikely, that there was an understanding between the police and PIs, but the man had been wrong before.

Well, I've come this far.

"I think… I think you should take a seat."

Dunbar scratched his chin, which had several days' worth of growth on it.

"Screech, you're a good guy and I'm forever indebted to Drake for his help getting my career started, but I can't do this. There's just too much—"

"I have the gun," Screech admitted. "I have the gun that killed Mark Magnusson."

Dunbar's eyes bulged.

"You *what*?"

A lump suddenly appeared in Screech's throat, making it difficult to swallow.

"Maybe we should go for a drive. I think we can help each other out, here."

***

"You have it here? On you?" Dunbar asked as they pulled away from the police station. Screech made it appear as if he was just driving aimlessly, but in fact, he was slowly making his way back toward MSG.

"No, not here—not with me. But I have it."

"You're playing a dangerous game, Screech."

It's not a game. It's Brock's life.

He said nothing.

"All right, all right, I'll bite. Let's say you have this gun in your possession and if you do, I'm guessing that Brock handed it to you. Or at least he told you where it is. Which means that you're convinced that he' s innocent."

Dunbar was a quick study, it appeared. But he fell just short of getting everything right.

"Which means that you want something in return. But like I told you before, Yasiv couldn't get Officer Kramer to drop the charges, so there's no way that I—"

"No, this isn't about Drake," Screech said quickly, making a left onto 8th Avenue. "This is about Brock."

"Ah, I see. A little you scratch my back, I scratch yours? That it? You give me the gun and… what? I tell you what we've got on Brock?"

This time, Screech didn't answer, and his silence didn't sit well with Dunbar.

"Screech, I'm this close to asking you to pull over, to putting the cuffs on you. I won't let you compromise this investigation. There's been too much corruption in the NYPD, and I won't add any more into the mix.

Screech bit his tongue.

"Talk to me, or I'll make you pull over."

Screech beat him to it; he slowed and parked at the side of the road. Dunbar raised his head and looked around, surprised that they were back at MSG. Almost immediately, a police officer waddled over, waving his hands frantically at them. Dunbar produced his badge and the man quickly retreated.

"I don't want to compromise the investigation. Like I said in the ring, if Brock's guilty, I'll help you put him behind bars. I'm not asking for you to do anything illegal, either."

Dunbar's eyes drifted back to Madison Square Garden.

"What are you asking for then, Screech?"

"*If* I give you the gun," Screech began slowly, choosing his words wisely, "if I give you the murder weapon that killed Mark Magnusson, all I want in return is to see the tapes from the night of the fight. I don't want to delete them, copy them, or change them. All I want to do is *see* them. Do we have a deal?"

Chapter 37

LEROY KNEW THAT SCREECH was right; owing Nick Petrazzino a favor was a mistake. But the man was downright scary, and they needed all the help they could get with Brock's case.

Besides, there was no guarantee that Nick would pull through, and if he didn't? There was no favor owed.

Things would go back to normal-*ish*.

What Leroy hadn't expected was, while trying to get as much information about the Page/Nolasco fight as he could from Reddit posts and videos uploaded to YouTube, to receive a call from a blocked number.

"Hello?"

"Meet me outside."

The line went dead, and Leroy stared at his phone for a second. Then he made his way over to the window and peered through the blinds.

There was a man with a ponytail smoking a cigarette in front of a black car with tinted windows.

It wasn't Nick Petrazzino, but there was no question that this man worked for him.

Leroy quickly dropped down out of sight.

"Shit."

He had an inkling to do one of two things: call Screech or to hide.

Both were shitty options, and both had consequences.

You got yourself into this mess, Leroy.

He opted for a third option.

"Are you Leroy Walker?" the man asked as he approached.

Leroy nodded, and the man took a final drag of his cigarette before flicking the butt to the asphalt.

"Get in the car. We're going for a ride."

It wasn't a question, but an order. Yet, Leroy hesitated. This was eerily similar to what had happened with the cops back in Tremont.

And in that scenario, he'd almost ended up dead.

"I think I'll walk."

The man with the ponytail started to nod as he opened the rear passenger door. Leroy knew that he should just keep on walking, but he couldn't resist the urge to look inside.

It was empty.

That's when the man cuffed him in the back of his head and before Leroy knew what was happening, he was thrust into the backseat.

"You don't fuckin' say no to me," the man growled as he got in beside him and shut the door. "When I say we're going for a ride, we're going for a ride."

Chapter 38

A NORMAL PERSON MIGHT have had a difficult time wading through some of the psychobabble that Dr. Fremont had used in her notes about Brock Page. But Hanna was far from an ordinary person, and her degree in psychology helped.

As she sat with her feet on the desk, combing through the doctor's notes and taking an occasional photograph with her cell phone, a truer picture of Brock Page started to come to the fore. And this image wasn't the same man who'd arrived at SLH in the middle of the night with a swollen face and gun in his hand asking, no, *begging* for help.

This Brock Page was entitled and stubborn. Hanna knew that most male athletes who had made it to The Show were alphas; it was nearly as integral to their success as their innate skill.

And Brock was no different.

Yet, as Hanna dug deeper, the man's superficial machismo started to unravel. Hidden in his words were issues of guilt — guilt at not supporting his old gym, Pike's Boxing Gym, when he made it big.

This gave Hanna pause.

A motive, she thought. *A failing gym, a disgruntled ex-coach.*

Hanna remembered what Leroy had told her about the spiteful owner, a man named Carl Severson, who had plucked both Shane and Brock off the streets. Carl had probably saved them from a life of crime.

And in return for his efforts?

Not even a public thank you, so far as Hanna could tell.

Brock also seemed racked with guilt over a relationship with one woman in particular. But as the minutes ticked by and Hanna scoured over Dr. Fremont's notes, this woman remained unnamed.

While earlier sessions were broader in scope, more recent meetings focused nearly entirely on this woman. Hanna knew she had to find her name, but there was just too much shit to wade through. She couldn't justify just taking the notes, either. Dr. Fremont may not have the best mind when it came to security, but she wasn't dumb.

It would take her all of three minutes before she realized that the woman who had robbed her was the wannabe tennis star who had also followed her to Nadine Nolasco's house.

And then Hanna wouldn't just be worried about Jimmy or Nick showing up at SLH, but the NYPD as well.

Starting to get frustrated now, Hanna flipped through the notes with the sole purpose of finding the damn woman's name.

Except it wasn't there; either Brock had never told her the name, or Dr. Fremont had decided not to write it down.

"Dammit," Hanna cursed, packing up the session notes and shoving them back into the cabinet. She used the letter opener to lock it again.

This adventure hadn't been a complete waste of time — Hanna now knew what Brock's primary preoccupation was — but it hadn't been as revealing as she'd hoped.

After pushing the chair back under the desk, Hanna started toward the door, already planning her next steps. But as she cast one final glance back into Dr. Fremont's office, her eyes kept getting drawn to the cabinet.

Only she wasn't focusing on the one that she'd just locked, but another.

"I should go," she told herself, but there was one more thing that she needed to check. "Just a quick peek. It's unlikely, it's unethical, but I have to know."

Hanna scooped up the letter opener and popped open the fourteenth cabinet. She quickly rifled through the patient names, and then stopped halfway through.

"Oh, you sly dog, you," she whispered.

Not only had Dr. Linda Fremont been treating Brock Page, but she very much appeared to be having sessions with his opponent as well.

As Hanna flipped through the session notes, the identity of the woman who Brock Page was all torn up about became painfully obvious.

Chapter 39

"YOU HAVE ONE HOUR, Screech," Detective Dunbar said as he opened the door to what looked like NASA's control room. "One hour, and then I'm coming to get you. And unless you have a signed confession from Brock, this is the last deal we make."

Screech stared at the wall of monitors, flabbergasted.

He wondered if one hour would be long enough to figure out how to work all of the equipment, let alone extract what he needed from video surveillance.

"And you're gonna wait until after I'm done here before you take the gun into evidence?" he asked, his eyes still locked on the array of monitors.

Screech was beginning to regret handing over the gun in the thick Ziploc bag.

"I'll wait."

"All right then," Screech said with a heavy sigh as he stepped into the control room.

He expected Dunbar to leave the room as they'd discussed, but when he didn't hear the door close, Screech turned around. Dunbar appeared pensive, distraught.

"What is it? I won't delete anything, and even if I did I bet MSG has everything backed up on the cloud."

Dunbar shifted his weight from one foot to the other.

"No, it's not that. Listen, what would you do if you knew someone was guilty of a crime, but still thought that this person did the right thing? That they were justified?"

The question was too ambiguous to answer, but Screech thought he knew what Dunbar was referring to.

Drake, he's talking about Drake.

Even when he'd still been a detective in the NYPD, Screech knew that Drake not only bent the rules but sometimes broke them. But he also got shit done and he put a lot of bad people behind bars.

Was it worth it? Was it just?

Maybe.

Probably.

"Yeah, that's what I think, too," Dunbar said, even though Screech hadn't answered him. "Okay, Screech, you've got one hour."

With that, the detective left Screech alone in the MSG control room.

"Let's play nice, now," he whispered. "Just play nice and give me what I need."

***

Screech spent the first ten minutes re-watching the short fight from every angle available, hoping to gain some insight into why Shane died. He paid close attention to Brock's gloves, trying to pick up on anything out of the ordinary. But they didn't seem to be modified in any way. Brock held them high and didn't labor when throwing punches. When they landed, however, Shane's head snapped back as if being struck by a cinder block.

Deciding that if Brock's gloves had been modified he wouldn't be able to tell from the video, Screech moved on. While most of the cameras showed different angles of the ring, there were also a handful that were dedicated to crowd watching. These mostly focused on the expensive seats, some of which were occupied by celebrities. Screech saw Anthony Kiedis of the Red Hot Chili Peppers, as well as Conor

McGregor, the enigmatic UFC champion, who had surrounded himself with a harem of women. The cameras continued to pan over the crowd and just as Screech was planning on turning his attention to backstage footage a blonde woman caught his eye.

He slowed down the footage and brought her face into focus.

"Huh," Screech said as he stared. His first instinct was that it was Shane Nolasco's wife, with his daughter sitting beside her, but he realized that that wasn't the case.

It was Dr. Linda Fremont and another woman he didn't recognize.

Screech snapped a quick photo with his cell phone and then backed the time stamp up all the way to hours before the actual fight took place.

He witnessed both Brock and Shane arriving at MSG sporting fancy suits, listening to headphones. TV footage cut away after a few seconds of this, but Screech managed to follow them all the way to their dressing rooms and inside with unaired material.

It was mostly boring fight preparation and Screech fast-forwarded most of it. He switched it back to real-time when Shane Nolasco took a seat on a chair and his coach started to tape his hands.

This is what I was looking for, Screech thought.

He watched the entire taping procedure with earnest, as did a member of the boxing commission. When his hands were taped, the appointee wrote his initials on the white fabric. He did the same on the tape that was used to secure Shane's boxing gloves.

Nothing seemed out of the ordinary to Screech, but Shane wasn't the one delivering deadly blows. It took some searching, but he eventually found the same footage, but from Brock's dressing room.

Screech paid even closer attention to this process but was disappointed in the end. The video was a carbon copy of the one from Shane's dressing room, with nothing out of the ordinary.

This doesn't make any sense.

Beckett's Savant had been certain that a boxer wearing twelve-ounce gloves couldn't deliver the damage that Shane Nolasco had sustained in the ring.

So, what the hell happened to him, then? Why the hell did his skull cave in? And who in god's name is responsible for his murder?

Chapter 40

AFTER BEING SHOVED INTO the back of the car, Leroy half expected to be bound and gagged, or maybe just have a dark hood thrown over his head.

Instead, the man with the ponytail tapped the driver on the shoulder and they drove away, leaving SLH in the distance.

Leroy tried to distract himself by looking outside, watching New York City pass by, but this made him nauseous. It wasn't like he didn't know where they were going, either.

They were headed to Little Italy.

Roughly fifteen minutes later, the car stopped outside of a restaurant and the man got out first.

In order to avoid being yanked out, Leroy quickly scooted across the seat and stepped onto the sidewalk.

The driver had parked outside of a squat building with red and white stripes painted onto the brick. The name above the large bay of windows read, in swooping, cursive letters, *Taglia's*.

Ponytail indicated the front door and Leroy headed directly for it. He was reaching for the handle when a human refrigerator came out.

Like the man in the car, he too had a ponytail, but his was braided and ended halfway down his massive back.

"Arms out," he ordered in a thick accent that Leroy couldn't place.

If he extended his arms any faster, they may have dislocated from their sockets. As the man frisked him, Leroy got a waft of strong cigarettes, the kind that old people who sat in rocking chairs on porches rolled by hand.

The man's sausage-like fingers squeezed the cell phone in his pocket and he told him to remove it.

Leroy did as he was told, and the man quickly slipped it into the inside pocket of a suit coat that looked more like a cape or a rug than something that one might wear to work.

"He'll give it back when you leave," original ponytail told him. "Now follow me."

Huh, at least I'll get to leave.

The interior of the restaurant was mostly unoccupied, with only a handful of patrons sitting at the circular tables that were covered with vintage table cloths.

It was like stepping into another era.

Leroy didn't get a chance to appreciate the archaic ambiance however, as he was quickly led through a set of swinging doors adjacent the kitchen.

"Keep up."

After passing through a hallway lined with photographs of people Leroy suspected might be famous but whom he didn't recognize, they passed through another set of doors.

These opened into a very different room from the one out front. There were TVs on nearly every wall airing either soccer games or what looked like stock tickers.

Seated at the main table was Nick Petrazzino, a glass of red wine in his hand, a cigar nestled in an ashtray in front of him. Across from him was a thin, balding man with round spectacles. Nick nodded to him, and the man scampered from the room without making eye contact.

"Leroy, so glad you could make it," Nick boomed in his trademark baritone voice.

Like I had a choice, Leroy thought.

Then to ponytail, he added, "You can go now, Oscar."

Oscar didn't look pleased by the order, and he shot a distasteful look at Leroy. He did, however, obey.

"Please, sit," Nick said, indicating the chair that the thin man had just vacated.

Leroy pulled the chair out and sat, still confused as to what, exactly, he was doing here.

"Would you like a glass of wine?" Nick asked, indicating an empty cup in the center of the table.

Take it, Leroy thought suddenly. *If I refuse the offer, he'll be offended.*

But what if it's poison? No, it can't be poison, he's drinking the same wine. But is he? Did you see him pour it? Where is the wine?

Leroy shook his head, trying to stop himself from doing what he always did in stressful situations: over think things.

"I'm okay, thanks—I'm underage."

You're also an idiot, he scolded himself.

Nick chuckled.

"In Italy, even the children have one glass of wine during special celebrations."

The comment set Leroy into panic mode again.

A celebration? This is a celebration? Should I congratulate him for something?

"But I respect your decision. *Saluti.*"

Nick sipped his wine and then leaned forward, something that Leroy noted was a sort of habit with him.

"I've been watching you for some time, Leroy."

What? Watching me? Why?

"Don't be alarmed, I'm watching everybody. But in particular, I watch people who I think I can help, and those who I think might be able to help me. You see, our late mayor, Ken Smith, was not good for business; he was good for his *own* business, sure, but not for ours. Now that he's gone, I predict that things are going to improve."

Business? What kind of business? The food and beverage business?

Leroy said nothing.

"And who better to team up with than those responsible for getting rid of Ken Smith?" Nick chuckled again and sipped his wine. "Don't you think?"

Leroy nodded, even though he wasn't sure what he was agreeing to. At least he finally understood why Nick had come to them in the first place. After all, SLH was just a start-up shop, one that was struggling to keep afloat. The mention of Ken Smith, along with the knowledge that DA Trumbo was likely the front runner to become the next mayor of New York City, put things into perspective. That, and the particular task that Nick had given SLH.

"That's why I came to you to retrieve the USB key. I'm not a petty man, but I do need to figure out if the people I intend to do business with are reliable and competent. Suffice it to say that so far I am *not* impressed."

Leroy finally found an opportunity to speak.

"We're working on it, we are, but the DA has surrounded himself by a security detail."

"Yes, I'm aware of that."

The man suddenly reached below the table and Leroy cringed, thinking that he was grabbing for a gun, that he would be executed for not retrieving the USB key sooner.

And when Nick pulled the trigger, the last thought that Leroy would have before his mind went dark would be of his brother and mom.

Of his promise to get out of the ghetto, to find a better life for himself.

And while he might've gotten out, his demise would be the same that had befallen Declan Walker not that long ago.

Chapter 41

HANNA WAS IN THE process of putting Shane's files back when she heard a sound and froze. Her first thought was that it was someone entering Sport Brain, and her heart started to pound in her chest. She instinctively gripped the letter opener tightly in her hand, and for a brief moment considered using it against whoever was coming.

But that was ridiculous. In addition to breaking and entering, she was going to be charged with what? Assault? Something worse?

She cursed herself for being so foolish, for taking so much time looking through Dr. Fremont's notes for a stupid name.

When Hanna didn't hear anything else, she figured she'd imagined the sound, or that it was coming from one of the adjacent businesses. Working as quickly and quietly as possible, she shoved the files in the cabinet, then locked it with the letter opener.

That was close, she thought as she reached for the door to Dr. Fremont's office.

Hanna immediately pulled her hand back just in time to avoid being struck by the door that started to open from the hallway.

Her eyes bulged, and she stepped to the side.

What the fuck!

Her gaze darted to the letter opener on the desk, but even if she wanted to use it now, there was no way to get it.

Hanna had one chance to get out of here without being seen, but it meant acting now.

She waited for the woman—for it was a woman, a blonde woman—to enter the office and walk toward the desk. Then Hanna slipped behind her, unseen, and was in the hallway before she'd even taken another breath. Staying as close to the wall as she could without touching it, she continued to move.

"Hello? Anyone there?"

Hanna pressed her back to the wall and blended in with the shadows. The woman—Dr. Fremont, it had to be Dr. Fremont—was most likely staring down the hallway, but Hanna knew better than to turn her head to look.

If she moved, there was no doubt that she'd be seen.

In her mind, Hanna counted to ten, then twenty. When there was no further query, she peeled herself away from the wall and slinked toward the front door.

By the time Hanna finally made it back to the safe confines of her VW, she was shaking so badly that she could barely shift the car into drive.

Chapter 42

JUST TO BE CERTAIN, Screech re-watched Brock getting his hands wrapped and gloves put on in slow motion.

But there was nothing interesting to see.

Next, he fast-forwarded the tape, reviewing all the footage from Brock's pre-fight warm-up.

And he almost missed it.

In fact, Screech *would* have missed it, if his eyes hadn't drifted to the time code in the bottom right-hand corner of the monitor.

Just as Brock was preparing himself to exit the locker room and take his stroll to the ring, the screen suddenly went black. At first, Screech thought that the camera had just been switched off, but the damn time code kept on ticking.

Three minutes later, Brock returned. Now he was standing at the door, knocking his gloves together, taking a series of deep breaths.

"What the hell?"

Everything else seemed as it was before.

Screech switched over to Shane's locker cam and, sure enough, before he took his walk to the ring, the video *also* went dark for approximately three minutes.

"What the hell is going on here?"

Someone had turned off the cameras. But who? Why?

Frantic now, knowing that Dunbar was due to return at any moment, Screech tried to pull up video footage from the hallway leading to the fighters' warm-up rooms. The problem was that everything was labeled by code, and not by name, and the legend was lost among a sea of papers on the desk. Screech spread them out, looking for something that would tell him which camera filmed the hallways.

"Where'd it go?" he grumbled.

I have to find out who was in the hallway when the cameras were shut off. I have to—

There was a knock at the door, and then Screech heard the deadbolt slide.

"Fuck!"

Screech started to snap pictures of the random sheets of papers, wondering why he hadn't documented everything the second he'd stepped into the room.

The door opened, but Screech just continued to move the pages around and snap more photos.

"The hour's up, Screech. I gotta get this gun into evidence, and you gotta get the hell out of here."

"Give me ten more minutes, Dunbar, please," Screech pleaded without looking up.

"No can do. The DA is coming here now, and you can't be around when he gets here. Not with Drake still on the loose."

Screech finally turned to look at the detective.

"I think I've found something. Both Brock and Shane's locker room cameras go dark right before they do their walk out."

Dunbar seemed unimpressed.

"They probably just shut 'em off. You gotta go, Screech."

"No, I don't think so. They came back on after a couple of minutes. Something happened, Dunbar, something happened in those few minutes."

Dunbar pushed his tongue into his cheek. Screech thought that he was breaking down, but then the detective shook his head.

"You gotta go."

"I need to see the tapes from the hallway. I need to know who entered their—"

Dunbar suddenly reached out and grabbed Screech's shoulder.

"Ten minutes! Give me ten minutes!"

Screech squirmed free, and in the process, his hand came down on a keyboard. A video started to play and both of them stared at the screen.

It would've been the greatest fluke on earth had the hallway video played, but Screech had never considered himself lucky. Instead, it was a shot of the front row of spectators, after Brock and Shane were already in the ring.

"You think I want to throw you in jail, Screech? Huh? Because I don't, but if you insist on—"

"Whoever entered Brock's room before the fight is responsible for killing Shane Nolasco, not Brock."

Dunbar reached for him again, but Screech pulled back and then moved toward the door.

"I'm going. For fuck's sake, I'm going!"

Dunbar moved between Screech and the computer just in case he changed his mind.

"I'm going!"

As he left the room, Screech's eyes were once again drawn to the monitor.

The video showed nothing but empty seats.

Empty seats... that had once been occupied.

He couldn't be absolutely certain, but Screech thought that this was where Dr. Fremont had been sitting earlier before Shane and Brock had made their way to the ring.

And now that they were getting ready to square off, the good doctor was nowhere to be found.

Chapter 43

IT WASN'T A GUN. Thank God, Nick Petrazzino didn't pull a gun out from beneath the table.

Leroy must've been sweating bullets because Nick laughed again. The man had a resonant chuckle that was somehow soothing and frightening at the same time.

"Relax, Leroy. As I said, I want to help those who can help me."

The implication of these words was not lost on Leroy.

"What's this?" he croaked, his eyes falling on the manila folder. When Nick just raised an eyebrow, Leroy cleared his throat and repeated the question. "What's this?"

"It's what you asked for."

Leroy drew a blank and Nick sighed.

"Sometimes I accept wagers from colleagues on upcoming sporting events. People I've dealt with before."

It finally clicked—the betting on the Page/Nolasco fight, the odds swinging in favor of a first round knock out.

Except something didn't make sense here.

"These are *your* betting lines?"

Nick eyed him suspiciously for a moment before a grin spread across his face.

"Ah, yes, you're wondering how a bet with me can alter the official betting lines posted online?"

Leroy nodded; that was exactly what he was thinking.

"Well, let's just say that if someone comes to me with a large sum of money and unwavering confidence, I may be inclined to reach out to other contacts and place a wager of my own. Contacts in Jersey or Vegas."

And that was all the confirmation that Leroy needed. He reached for the folder and started to open it when a meaty hand came down and kept it closed.

"Not here, not now."

Leroy nodded.

"Thank you," he said, rising to his feet. Oscar appeared out of nowhere and approached Leroy from behind.

"I help you, you help me," Nick repeated. "I need that USB."

That was a job, and this is a favor.

But Leroy was no longer upset by this realization. If anything, he was excited. Excited, because he was onto something.

"Now, Mr. Buglioni will take you home." Nick stood and held out his hand. Leroy tried to shake it, but his dark mitt was swallowed whole. "I'll be in touch."

With that, Oscar Buglioni guided Leroy out of the private room.

They walked together down the hallway and then through the restaurant. Leroy didn't see any of the photos on the wall this time; his eyes were focused solely on the folder.

He couldn't wait to look inside.

"Your phone," the human refrigerator said as they stepped into the failing sun.

Leroy took it from the man and slipped it into his pocket.

"Thanks," he said absently.

Oscar didn't need to throw him into the car as he'd done outside SLH; Leroy veritably sprinted to the backseat. And the second the door was closed behind him, he flipped the folder open and started searching for familiar names.

"Well, I hope it was worth it," Oscar grunted beside him.

Leroy's finger shot out and he tapped one name in particular.

Then he started to smile, not just a regular grin, but a smile that showed off his pearly whites. A smile that he hadn't experienced in months.

"Oh, it was," Leroy said in a voice just louder than a whisper. "It was very much worth it."

PART IV

Placing Bets

Chapter 44

"**BROCK WAS *WHAT*?**"

Hanna nodded.

"You heard me the first time. Brock page was sleeping with Nadine Nolasco—Shane Nolasco's wife."

Screech was floored. He couldn't believe what his partner was telling him. Brock had come to them pleading for help, begging them with tears in his eyes, and they'd fallen for it.

While the entire time, Brock was sleeping with Shane's wife, which amounted, in Screech's estimation, to one thing: motive.

"That's what they were fighting about," Leroy said softly.

Screech's eyes went wide; another bombshell.

"Wait a second, you think that Shane *knew* Brock was sleeping with his wife?"

Leroy started to answer, but Hanna interrupted.

"No, no way. Look, Shane might've been depressed, in the twilight of his career, and he was no longer the alpha male of the pride, but he was still a professional athlete—a boxer. There's no way in hell that he would've confronted his friend about sleeping with his wife and left in a huff. He would've punched Brock in the face. And remember, it was Brock who tried to push Shane, and not the other way around."

Screech squinted at Hanna.

"Shane was depressed?"

Hanna squirmed, and Screech pressed harder.

"How could you possibly know that, Hanna? How could you know that Shane was depressed?"

"I've got a psychology degree, remember?"

While factually correct, this reasoning was complete and utter bullshit, and everyone in the room knew it.

Including Hanna.

"Hanna, where did you go this afternoon? You didn't—"

"Hey, you did what you had to do, found out what you could, and I did the same," Hanna said defensively. "We're a team, remember."

Screech sighed and shook his head. He only had so much anger to go around, and right now most of it was reserved for Brock Page.

"What about you, Leroy? Please tell me some good news."

"Well, I've got something… don't know if it can be considered good news, though," the man said as he produced a folder.

Inside were several sheets of printed pages, but Leroy was only interested in the first one. He held it out to Screech. On the page was a list of names, along with columns and dollar amounts. Screech looked at it for a moment then looked to Leroy for an explanation.

"What is all this stuff?"

"Those are bets—the names of people who put money on the Page/Nolasco fight and what they thought the outcome was going to be. And look who just happened to pick Brock to knock Shane out in the first."

Screech tried again to figure out the list, but the numbers just got blurred into an alphabet soup. Sensing his confusion, Leroy reached out and tapped a line near the top of the page.

"Linda Fremont," Screech read out loud. "Wait—no, this can't be."

"Oh, it is."

"You're telling me that Dr. Fremont put—wow—she put $100,000 on Brock Page to knock out Shane Nolasco in the first round. Is this for real?"

"Yup," Leroy confirmed with a hint of pride. "It's real all right."

Screech committed the betting line to memory, then slowly placed the sheet of paper on his desk. Then he leveled an icy stare at Leroy.

"Where did you get this?"

Leroy averted his eyes as Hanna had done moments ago.

"Leroy, where did you get this?" Screech demanded.

"I didn't have much of a choice," Leroy replied. It was times like these that Screech had to remind himself that Leroy was only a nineteen-year-old kid.

Sure, he'd seen a lot, been through more shit in those nineteen years than most dealt with in a lifetime. And yet, most of his actions were excusable, and could be chalked up to naivety.

But this? Making a deal with Nick Petrazzino of all people? This was inexcusable.

"How could you? I specifically told you not to deal with that man. I said don't—"

"Screech, c'mon," Hanna pleaded. "It's not his fault."

This was the final straw. Screech was fed up with all the lies and deception, from clients and business partners both.

Why can't they see that I'm trying to help them here? Why can't they just listen?

Seething, he looked to the door, and for the first time since moving into this fancy new office, he considered that he might be better off if SLH Investigations lost a few more letters.

Shit, maybe they should have just folded after Drake abandoned them.

"I'm sorry, but I didn't have a choice," Leroy said, trying to justify his actions.

"You always have a choice," Screech whispered.

He wasn't thinking about Nick Petrazzino anymore or even Dr. Linda Fremont. He was thinking about the night of the silent auction at the Loomis Estate, the night that had changed everything.

"Screech? You okay?" Hanna asked, sliding off her desk and reaching for him. "You're shaking."

Screech cleared his throat.

"I'm fine. Just tired," he lied. He wasn't fine and doubted he ever would be again.

"Maybe we should take a break. We're all tired and some rest might help us think clearly, approach this from a new angle."

Hanna, the sudden voice of reason.

Screech closed his eyes and shook his head.

"No, I'm okay—we don't have time to rest." He took a deep breath and then stared at Hanna. "Dunbar let me see the tapes, just like you said he would. There are three minutes where the cameras go black right before Brock and Shane head to the ring. Whoever came into Brock's dressing room then helped him kill Shane."

As he let this settle in their minds, Screech got to his feet and headed toward the door.

"Where you going?" Leroy asked.

"To pay Brock a visit, ask him for the truth. The *whole* truth this time."

"What about us? What do you want us to do?"

Screech started walking again and this time, he didn't turn around.

"Stay out of prison and stay out of the morgue. Other than that, you two are on your own."

Chapter 45

SCREECH STORMED INTO 62ND precinct, ignoring the stares from confused-looking police officers. Even when the woman behind the desk asked him in increasingly louder tones what he needed, what he was doing here, Screech just kept his head down and moved forward.

He might've even continued walking until someone put him in cuffs if he hadn't noticed Roger Schneiderman standing off to one side talking to a uniformed officer.

The lawyer looked even more tired now than he had at 2 a.m. when Screech had called him to take on Brock's case. Clearly, he'd heard the news about the gun that had killed Mark Magnusson being admitted into evidence.

"Where is he?" Screech demanded.

Roger said something to the officer, who nodded and made his way to the back.

"Screech, things are—"

"Where is he?" Screech demanded again.

Roger looked around, clearly uncomfortable, but eventually answered, trying to keep his voice down.

"He's in holding. But they're going to move him to County in a couple of hours. Tomorrow morning he'll stand before a judge and enter his plea."

"I need to see him."

Roger reached out and grabbed Screech's arm and pulled him close.

The man's breath was stale, and he smelled of sweat.

At least I'm not the only one who isn't sleeping, Screech thought.

"He's not doing so hot," Roger whispered. "Brock's really not doing well.

"No shit," Screech hissed. "Facing twenty-five to life will do that to a man."

Roger suddenly pulled Screech to a more private area. If it hadn't been for the look on the man's face, Screech would have resisted.

"No, Screech, it's not just that. He was attacked last night— three times."

This was the last thing that Screech expected to hear.

"*What?* He was attacked in holding? What the hell happened?"

Roger's beady eyes glanced around the room before answering.

"Everyone knows who he is, and they all want to make a name for themselves by taking out the champ. And Brock won't even defend himself. Look, I managed to get him a cell by himself, so he could sleep a little, but if they move to County... it's only gonna get worse. Someone's gonna hurt him, hurt him bad."

Screech was having a difficult time processing all of this.

The WBA and WBC Super Middleweight champion was getting attacked in prison? And he refused to defend himself?

He shook his head.

"I need to see him," Screech said, his tone softening. "I really need to talk to him."

Roger Schneiderman nodded.

"Come with me."

***

Roger hadn't been exaggerating when he'd said that Brock was in rough shape. Screech figured that the lack of sleep had made them all worse for wear, but Brock had been hit particularly hard—both figuratively and literally.

The man had fresh bruises on his face, and the cut on his lip, which should have scabbed over by now, leaked freely.

But despite his injuries, the man perked up when Screech approached him in the interview room.

"Thank God," Brock nearly gasped. "Please tell me you've got some good news."

Seeing the man this way inspired feelings of pity in Screech, but then he remembered Shane Nolasco and Mark Magnusson and these feelings vanished.

"Good news? *Good* news? They've got the gun now, Brock, and tomorrow you're going in front of a judge."

Brock rested his elbow on the table and gripped his forehead.

"I'm fucked—it's over, it's all over."

"Yeah, it is. And it's your fault, Brock. It's your fault because you haven't been telling me the truth."

Screech could sense Roger tense behind him, but he didn't care. He was angry, angry at everyone.

Brock looked up.

"What? What do you mean?"

"Exactly what I said: you've been lying to me since the beginning."

Confusion washed over Brock's battered face.

"I don't know what—"

"Why didn't you tell me that you were sleeping with Shane's wife? Huh?"

Brock's shoulders immediately sagged, and the man's muscled physique seemed to liquefy.

Behind him, Screech heard Roger gasp, a reaction that, under different circumstances, would have been comical.

"Why didn't you tell me?" Screech pressed harder.

Brock took a deep, shuddering breath.

"I didn't think... I didn't think it was relevant," he almost whispered.

Screech gawked.

"You didn't think it was relevant? You didn't think that telling me that you were sleeping with the wife of the man whose brains you spilled all over MSG was *relevant?* Either you've taken one too many blows to the head, Brock, or it's time that you let someone else take over in the thinking department."

Chapter 46

"HOW *DID* YOU FIND out that information about Shane and Brock?" Leroy asked.

Hanna gave him a sly grin.

"A girl never tells," she replied. "But what Mr. Grumpy Pants didn't give me a chance to say, is that there's more to Dr. Fremont's story than meets the eye. The woman has some serious financial problems: you should've seen the way she snatched the money from me only to immediately hand it over to the repo man or whoever he is. So, the question now is how does she get a hundred grand to bet on the fight?"

Leroy mulled this over before spouting off ways that he might come up with cash if his situation got desperate enough.

"Sell a car, maybe? Shoes? Borrow money? Drugs?"

Hanna shook her head to all of these.

"She was still driving her car and that's a lot of shoes."

Leroy chewed on his thumbnail as he considered other options. Something that Nick had said at *Taglia's* suddenly occurred to him.

"You know what? Maybe Dr. Fremont didn't have the money."

Hanna's eyes narrowed.

"What do you mean?"

"Well, it's something that Nick said in passing when he handed over the betting sheet. Something about how he only accepts bets from people he knows, people he's dealt with before."

"So… maybe Dr. Fremont didn't have to put any cash up because Nick knew—or thought—that she was good for it based on their past dealings?" Hanna said, finishing the thought for him.

"A psychiatrist for athletes getting inside information and placing bets based on that info? I'd buy it. Except she sucks at it."

Hanna shrugged.

"A couple bad bets, some fluky outcomes? Things can change quickly."

"Yeah, but Dr. Fremont won *this* bet—won big time. Why so desperate for cash, then?"

"I don't know… hasn't collected yet? Wants to wait for things to cool down? Think about it; you make a bet of this size and the person you pick to lose dies in the ring? That's damn suspicious. I would definitely wait a while before collecting my profits." Hanna scratched her head before continuing. It was almost as if she was talking to herself now, thinking out loud. "Yeah, but you should've seen her when I was waving the cash around. She was *despo.* Dr. Fremont didn't look like someone who was just waiting to collect a windfall of profits."

Leroy sighed.

"And none of this answers the real question."

"Which is?"

"How the hell Dr. Fremont knew the outcome of the fight in the first place. It's one thing to use inside knowledge of the fighter's mental status to guess what was going to happen, but something this specific? And Shane *dies*? You gotta have some big-time balls to put up a hundred grand you don't have with someone like Nick Petrazzino on a hunch."

"And now we've come full circle."

They fell silent after Hanna's last comment. There were so many elements to this case that didn't make sense that it was difficult knowing where to start.

But the beginning was always a good place.

"Let me ask you something, Leroy. You're Brock or Dr. Fremont or whoever, and you want Shane to go down in the first round and never get up. You can't shoot him, can't drug him, can't rough him up beforehand, soften his skull that sort of thing, because he has to pass his physical in order to fight. All you have is a set of boxing gloves. How do you do it?"

"And the gloves have to be around the same size and weight?"

"Yep. Gotta look the same and behave the same—can't have spikes or whatever shooting out of the padding."

Leroy took a deep breath and thought back to his chemistry classes. What could inflict enough damage to cause a man's skull to collapse as Shane's had?

He snapped his fingers and opened his eyes.

"Liquid."

Hanna's lips twisted into some facsimile of a sneer.

"Liquid? C'mon. Like fucking water gloves? I don't think so. The man's skull was caved in."

Leroy shook his head.

"No, not a regular liquid. A non-Newtonian liquid."

Hanna continued to stare.

"*Ooookay*, now."

"No, seriously," Leroy continued, spinning around in his chair and pulling himself up to his computer. "They're using this stuff for military applications, like armor. Basically, it's a fluid up until the time of impact and then the molecules lock together to form a solid."

Hanna blinked.

"What?"

"Yeah, they're also called shear thickening or dilatant fluids."

"And you think this is what someone put in Brock's gloves?"

Leroy shrugged.

"Injected, maybe. I don't know if this is what was really used, but this is how I would do it."

Hanna still seemed dubious, but in the end, gave in.

"Okay, okay. So, then where would I get some of this stuff?"

Leroy typed away at his keyboard for a moment, before smiling and turning the monitor to Hanna.

"There's only one place in New York: Isaac Innovations."

Hanna slid off the desk and started toward the door.

"What? Wait a second! Where are you going?" Leroy asked, confused.

"To talk to this fucking Isaac guy, where do you think?"

Chapter 47

"**WHAT ELSE HAVE YOU** deemed to be irrelevant, Brock? Maybe that you were the one who pulled the trigger? Who shot and killed Mark Magnusson? Maybe he found out about your affair and—"

"No," Brock suddenly shouted. "No. I didn't kill him. Me and Mark didn't always get along, but I didn't kill him."

"Then who did? And, another thing, why didn't you tell me that both you and Shane were seeing Dr. Fremont? Huh?"

Brock leaned back from the table.

"What? Shane was seeing Linda?"

"Sure was."

"I didn't… I had no idea. I've been seeing Dr. Fremont for years now. You sure?"

Screech pictured Hanna's face when he'd asked her where she'd acquired her information.

"Yeah, he was. Highly unethical on Dr. Fremont's part, especially right before your fight."

"Well, I didn't tell you, because I didn't fucking know."

Screech glanced at Roger Schneiderman over his shoulder, who held his palms up.

Fucking useless.

"Speaking of Dr. Fremont, did she know that you were sleeping with Shane's wife?"

Brock hesitated but eventually nodded.

"Yeah, I think so. I mean, I never mentioned her name but Linda's a smart woman."

"What about Shane? Did he know? Is that what you guys fought about at Pike's Boxing Gym a week ago?"

Brock's jaw literally fell open.

"*What?* How did you—"

"Damn it, Brock, you hired me to figure out what the hell happened to your friend, but all you've done so far is keep secrets, make my job as difficult as possible. It's almost as if you don't want to get off."

Brock stared at his hands.

"Maybe I don't," he whispered.

Screech suddenly slammed his fist down on the table and the man across from him jumped.

"What the fuck's going on here, Brock? I told you that if you're guilty, I will take everything I find out to the cops. I *told* you that."

"Easy, Screech," Roger warned.

"You take it easy," he shot back over his shoulder. "Brock, what's going on?"

Brock suddenly leaped to his feet and this time it was Screech who was startled. Jaws and fists clenched, the incensed man growled.

"I didn't kill my manager, but I killed Shane, all right? I don't know how, but I did—Millions of people saw me do it. And I deserve to be punished. Shane was a good man, a friend, and I fucked him over. I slept with his wife and then I killed him in the ring."

Brock suddenly reared back as if to throw a punch and Screech, so surprised by this sudden outburst, could only stare.

Thankfully, Roger wasn't as shell-shocked.

"Guard! *Guard!*" the lawyer shouted as he banged on the door behind them. The guard instantly appeared and started to unlock the door.

This sound seemed to have a profound effect on Brock. Perhaps it was the realization that he was locked up and might remain that way for the rest of his natural life, or maybe it was the weight of his own admission. Either way, the man backed down.

"I'm sorry—*I'm sorry*. Shane didn't know I was sleeping with his wife; he had no idea. But he knew somebody was. He knew she was cheating on him, but he didn't know who. He called me to meet up at Pike's gym to ask for advice… shit, he wanted to back out of the fight, man, wanted to focus on her." Brock broke down. "*I* convinced him to fight. I was the… I was the one who told him he had to… and I was the one who killed him…"

The guard entered the interview room and stepped between Roger and Screech, and a now weeping Brock.

"What else are you not telling me, Brock?"

"Nothing. I've told you everything. Now please, just leave me alone."

As Screech eyed his client up and down, the feelings of pity started to return. As did the unwavering notion that Brock really was innocent. Not of sleeping with his friend's wife and not of delivering the blow that ended up taking his life.

But of homicide.

"You gotta leave now," the guard instructed. "I'm taking him to County."

"Just a second," Screech said. "One second."

The guard looked to Roger, who nodded. Then he stepped to one side but remained poised and at the ready, in case Brock lashed out again.

"Something happened right before the fight—before you left the locker room."

"What do you mean?"

"Three minutes before you walked to the ring, the cameras went dark. Who came to visit you during that time?"

Brock scrunched his nose, which caused the split in his lip to open up again.

"I don't know… nobody. I was prepping for my fight, thinking about—wait, wait," Brock's eyes suddenly widened.

"What?"

"Linda visited me—Dr. Fremont. I got her and her assistant tickets to the fight, and she came to talk to me right before I went to the ring. I thought it was strange, and she said something about how her lucky number was four or something. I had no idea what the hell she was talking about."

Screech frowned.

"You sure? She mentioned the number four?"

"Yeah… three times. It was fucking weird."

Screech was going to chastise the man for once again not telling him everything, but Brock had already been through enough. Instead, he thought about the betting list that Leroy had obtained from Nick Petrazzino.

Why would Dr. Fremont mention the number four, when she'd put so much money on the first round.

"One more thing, Brock. Was this normal? Did Dr. Fremont usually come to visit you before your fight?"

Brock shook his head.

"No, no way. I've gotten her tickets before, a couple of times, but this is the first time she ever came into the locker room."

One hell of a coincidence, Screech thought. *The very first time she visits you in the locker room is also the very first time you kill somebody in the ring.*

Chapter 48

FOR THE SECOND TIME that day, Hanna was impersonating someone else. Earlier, it had been Natalia Abramovsky and now it was Natalia Spectre. She was wearing the power suit she'd worn when she'd pick-pocketed the DA and appropriated the same mannerisms, feelings of self-importance.

Hanna waltzed through the front doors of Isaac Innovations like she owned the place, knowing that the way one carried oneself did much more for an image than any words could.

Unlike Sport Brain, there were no chairs for visitors and the desk was a simple cubicle with a computer monitor and phone on it. Behind the desk sat a man with orange skin and a chinstrap beard straight out of nineteen-ninety-six.

"How may I help you, ma'am?" Fake and Bake asked in a high-pitched voice.

"I'm here to pick up an order of Liquid Armor."

The man's face contorted into perhaps the most exaggerated expression that Hanna had ever seen.

"Uh, excuse me?"

"Liquid Armor. I placed an order last week and now I'm here to pick it up."

"What are you talking about?"

Hanna scowled.

"You don't make Liquid Armor here? This isn't Isaac Innovations?"

"Well, yeah, to both, uh, but… gimme a sec."

The man picked up the phone and dialed a single number. Then he turned his chair back to her and spoke in a hushed tone, but Hanna could still clearly hear what he was saying.

"Some woman is here... says she ordered Liquid Armor. Yeah, I didn't even think we were selling it yet."

Things were definitely not going as planned, yet Hanna was still gathering valuable intel.

"Yeah, uh, I'll tell her. But maybe you could come talk to her? Okay, okay. See you soon."

The man hung up and then smiled at Hanna.

"I think there's been some confusion. Can you just wait here a moment? My manager is going to come talk to you."

Hanna nodded, but then glanced at her watch as if to say, *time is money, bitch; hurry the fuck up.*

Less than a minute later, a tall, birdlike man emerged from behind a thick metal door. He made sure to close it securely before approaching her.

"Yes, Miss..."

"Spectre."

He was wearing a white lab coat with the words *Isaac Institute* written on the chest.

Well, at least I'm in the right place.

"Yes, Mrs. Spectre—"

"Miss Spectre."

The man's Adam's apple bobbed.

"Y-yes, Miss Spectre, there seems to be some confusion. We're not actively accepting orders for Liquid Armor."

Hanna shook her head.

"That's impossible. I placed an order last week."

"Y-y-you did? Where? We don't have a website or—"

"Dr. Linda Fremont told me about it, and she gave me the order form."

Hanna stared intently at the scientist as she said the psychiatrist's name, hoping to see a flash of recognition cross his features.

Her heart sunk when the man showed a blank.

"I'm really sorry, Miss Spectre, but I don't know a Dr. Fremont. Does she... does she work for the NSF?"

Hanna had no idea what the NSF was but decided to run with it.

"Yes, of course. As do I. Now I would like to know why our order hasn't been fulfilled."

"NSF? The National Science Foundation?"

Whoops.

"You know what," Hanna began, backing toward the door. "I'm going to have a little chat with Dr. Fremont. Figure this out. Then I'll be back."

"Uh, yeah, uh, uh, o-o-kay."

Hanna opened the door to leave when her gaze fell on the man behind the desk. Where previously his face had been twisted into some sort of pretzel, it had changed now.

It was flaccid.

The man's eyes were darting about, too, as if he wasn't just uncomfortable, but worried.

As Hanna made her way back to her car, she started to smile.

The manager might not know who Dr. Fremont is, but she had a sneaking suspicion that Fake and Bake just might.

Chapter 49

SCREECH WAITED OUTSIDE THE interview room until Brock had been shackled and taken back to his holding cell. Then he turned to a weary-looking Roger Schneiderman.

"I think Brock needs to go to the infirmary," Screech observed.

"Naw, he'll be alright. County, on the other hand, is—"

Screech shook his head.

"No, I think his nose is broken. It wasn't like that before. He should be checked out."

Roger looked at Screech.

"His nose has been—"

Screech snarled.

"—broken recently. He needs to go to the infirmary to get it checked out."

When it still didn't appear as if Roger was catching on, Screech basically spelled it out for him.

"Brock can't go to County, because he needs to see the doctor and be held for twenty-four hours under observation."

A lightbulb seemed to go off behind Roger's beady eyes.

"Oh… oh, oh, yeah. You're right. But usually, they only keep you for twelve hours… is that enough time for you… I mean, him… to… heal?"

What a fucking idiot.

"Twelve hours is not much time for a broken nose to heal, but with the proper treatment, and a little luck, the doctors might come up with a solution."

Roger nodded, and Screech started to make his way back to the front of the station.

Twelve hours really wasn't that much time. He hoped that Hanna and Leroy had come up with something that further implicated Dr. Fremont.

Something that they could use to convince Detective Dunbar and the DA that Brock was innocent.

Screech would have walked right by the occupied holding cell if it hadn't been for the four armed guards standing in front of it.

That's the type of security that Brock needs, he thought, picturing the man's wounds. In an organized fight, Brock would make mincemeat of even the most hardened inmate. But jail was different; there were no rules and there was no standing eight count.

He might still have a chance if he fought back. But all the fight seemed to have gone out of Brock.

"Maybe you should spread the security out a little bit," Screech grumbled as he passed the cell.

None of the officers even looked at him, but the man in the cell raised his eyes.

"Screech?"

Screech turned to face the man who'd spoken his name and then froze.

Sergeant Henry Yasiv was nearly unrecognizable. He'd lost a considerable amount of weight, making his face appear hollow and his skin was gray. It looked as if he hadn't shaved in a month.

"Yasiv?"

The man stared at him with rheumy eyes.

"Jesus Christ, how long have you been here?" Screech asked.

"I didn't do this," he said. "I didn't kill the reverend or his wife."

It was so strange to see the once proud police officer so disheveled and caged like this, that Screech was having a hard time processing the scene.

"I didn't kill them, and I didn't kill Captain Loomis."

Screech was at a loss for words. He jumped when an arm suddenly draped over his shoulder.

"It's probably best if you don't talk to him," Roger whispered in his ear.

The man tried to pull Screech away from the cell, but he remained rooted in place.

"I didn't kill them," Yasiv exclaimed, rising to his feet. "I didn't kill anybody."

The prisoner moved to the front of the cell, which got one of the guards' attention. He turned and ordered Yasiv to sit back down.

"I didn't kill anybody!" Yasiv suddenly shouted. He gripped the bars in both hands and then seemed to try to squeeze his face through—he looked like some sort of wild animal. "Screech, tell them, tell them that I didn't kill anybody. *Tell them!*"

The guard lashed out with his nightstick, rapping it off Yasiv's knuckles hard enough to cause an echo. Yasiv cried out and immediately backed away from the bars, clutching his injured hand.

"I said, sit the fuck down."

Roger pulled harder now, and Screech was reluctantly drawn back into the waiting area of 62nd precinct.

"Poor guy has no chance," Roger grumbled.

Screech finally rid himself of the cloak of shock and grabbed Roger by the shoulders.

"I want you to represent him."

"What?"

Screech squeezed even harder.

"Henry Yasiv—I want you to represent him."

Roger shook his head.

"Yeah, I don't think that's a good idea. I gotta work with these cops, and Yasiv isn't—

"I'll pay. I'll pay you whatever you want," Screech said. "Whatever you want."

"I—I can't. That would be the end of—"

"*Whatever you want!*" Screech shouted.

Roger looked around at the handful of officers who had started to stare.

"*Whatever—*"

"Okay, okay," Roger said, finally relenting. "Just let go of my arms… you're—you're hurting me."

Chapter 50

"HI," HANNA SAID WITH a smile. "Remember me?"

The man with the fake tan put the menthol cigarette in his mouth and lit it. Then he exhaled a cloud of smoke in Hanna's direction.

"Sure, you're the crazy bitch who wanted to buy Liquid Armor."

Hanna winced at the word bitch.

"That's me, crazy bitch Natalia Spectre. I couldn't help but notice that when I mentioned Dr. Fremont's name, you seemed to recognize it."

The man took another drag, this time exhaling out of the corner of his mouth.

"Never heard of her."

"You sure?"

The man rolled his eyes.

"Get out of here."

"Maybe you just don't want to tell me, because I'm a crazy bitch. But maybe you want to tell my friend?"

The man raised a manicured eyebrow.

"What the hell are you talking about?"

"My friend—his name is Tyrone."

"What?"

Leroy suddenly appeared from around the side of the building, a snarl on his face. It was so Hollywood that Hanna nearly laughed.

But it worked. Fake and Bake took one look at Leroy and the cigarette nearly fell out of his mouth.

"Tyrone, why don't you come here. Ask him—"

"Fuckin' hell," the man mumbled. "Look, I don't know who this Dr. Fremont is, seriously. But I might have sold a little bit of Liquid Armor to some blond lady who seemed desperate."

And that would be Dr. Fremont, Hanna thought.

"It was just some test compound that we were going to throw out anyhow. There, you happy?"

Leroy flinched at the man, and he recoiled. This time, the cigarette fell to the ground.

"Fuck."

"Thank you very much for your help, Oompa Loompa," Hanna said, gesturing for Leroy to follow her back to the car. Once inside, they watched the nervous-looking secretary light another smoke.

"I gotta give it to you, Leroy, I was skeptical. Non-Newtonian fluid? Ha. Man, Screech is gonna lose his mind when we tell him."

When Leroy didn't answer, Hanna looked at him.

"What? What's wrong? It worked… we have Dr. Fremont dead to rights. Means, motive, and opportunity. Brock is going free."

Leroy scrunched his nose.

"Tyrone? Seriously?"

Hanna chuckled; she couldn't help it.

"What? Leroy just doesn't carry the same… intimidation factor."

"You know what? When this case is over, you and Screech are going for some sensitivity training. This is getting ridiculous."

Chapter 51

"**HE DIDN'T DO IT,**" Screech said. "Brock didn't do it. He admitted to sleeping with Shane's wife and he admitted to the fight, but Shane didn't know it was him. He also said that it was Dr. Fremont who visited him before the fight. But now we've got another problem—they're going to ship him to County and people are already laying their claim, taking shots at him, trying to make a name for themselves. Roger is getting him checked out in the infirmary, but after Brock goes before the judge tomorrow morning, he's going to County. Nothing we can do about it."

He expected to see concern on Hanna and Leroy's faces, but they seemed strangely excited.

"What's going on? Why are you looking at me like that?"

"I'll let Leroy answer that," Hanna said.

Leroy cleared his throat.

"Don't you mean Tyrone?"

Hanna laughed, but Screech just stared.

"Enough fucking around. Did you not hear what I said about Brock?"

"Yeah, sorry," Leroy muttered. "But I think we figured out how Shane died. There's this company called Isaac Innovations that is working on a Liquid Armor product. It's a liquid that becomes solid upon impact. I think it was injected into Brock's gloves and that's why his punches were so powerful."

"What? Really? How do you—"

"Because the little prick behind the desk said he sold some to none other than Dr. Fremont," Hanna interjected.

Screech exhaled loudly.

"Wow. She set this all up, didn't she? Planned it all from the beginning. Mark must have found out about it, and she killed him, too."

He was just thinking out loud, but it seemed plausible. But not all pieces in this puzzle were neatly coming together.

"Why the long face?" Hanna asked. "We got her."

Screech shook his head.

"Brock said that Dr. Fremont kept repeating the fourth when she visited him. I was certain that she was trying to influence him into taking out Shane in the fourth round. I was sure of it."

"Maybe he misheard, or it meant nothin'," Leroy offered.

"Yeah, maybe," Screech said, but he wasn't convinced. There was definitely something about this that he just wasn't seeing.

"Well, there's one thing I know for certain," Hanna said.

"And what's that?"

"That it's time to pay Dr. Linda Fremont another visit, don't you think?"

Chapter 52

"**WHAT DO YOU MEAN** I don't get to go? You should've seen how smug she was last time… I wanna return the favor."

Screech shook his head; he wasn't going to back down on this, either. If Dr. Fremont saw Hanna coming, she might panic, run, or do something even more serious.

That was a risk he wasn't prepared to take.

"I'm going," Hanna said defiantly.

"No, you're not. But there's someone I need you to go see."

"Nice try, but I'm not up for a milk run. Leroy, back me up on this. We're a team and—"

Leroy surprised them both by shaking his head.

"I'm with Screech on this one. It doesn't make sense for you to go. If she recognizes you, it could ruin everything."

Hanna made a face, but before she could stake her claim, Screech tried to stem her anger.

"We are a team, and that's why you can't go. And it's not a milk run I want you to do. We still don't know how Shane's wife fits into all of this, and why Dr. Fremont went to visit her after Shane died. I need you to go talk to her."

This seemed to interest Hanna, made apparent by the fact that she stopped shaking her head.

"Fine," she said with a pout. "But don't expect me to get all weepy and huggy with her."

"Hanna, she lost her husband—"

"Whatever."

Screech let it go. Hanna had already proven that she was a chameleon, that she could become whoever she needed to be to extract as much information as possible.

He expected her to do the same with Nadine Nolasco.

"What about me?" Leroy asked.

"Well, Tyrone, I'm gonna need some muscle in case Dr. Fremont gets out of line."

Leroy smiled.

"All right, you got me there."

"How 'bout you go wait in the car—I'll be out in a minute."

Leroy didn't suffer from the same ego as Hanna and didn't bat an eye at the request even though it was obvious that Screech just wanted to speak to her alone.

"Make it quick. Got a dominoes game with the homies in the alley in an hour or so."

Screech waited for Leroy to leave, before turning to Hanna.

"I need that gun," he said flatly.

Hanna made a face.

"I thought you gave it Dunbar. I thought that you traded it for access to the cameras at MSG?"

"Not that gun, the other one… the one from the Loomis Estate. I saw Sergeant Yasiv in prison, and he's in rough shape. I *need* that gun."

Hanna's expression became a scowl.

"And what would you do if you had that gun, Screech? Hmm? Would you just hand it over, with your prints on it? The only way to exonerate Yasiv is to implicate yourself, and you know it."

She was right. As much as he hated to admit it, Hanna was right.

"There has to be another way."

"Yeah, there is, but it doesn't involve the gun. Besides, I have no idea where it is."

Screech relented, but there was nothing else he could do about Yasiv's situation now.

"Well, we need something in case Dr. Fremont decides to get violent."

Without a word, Hanna went to her desk, pulled her gun out and checked that the magazine was loaded. Then she tossed it at Screech.

"Jesus, Hanna," he exclaimed, barely catching the gun before it fell to the floor.

"I hope you know how to use that thing because Dr. Fremont killed Mark Magnusson with one shot."

Their eyes met, and Hanna bowed her head.

"Sorry," she grumbled.

"That's alright. It's not like I'm actually going to use it."

Screech couldn't help but think that he'd never intended to use it at the Loomis Estate, either, and look how that turned out.

Chapter 53

THE THING THAT HANNA regretted most about giving her gun to Screech was that it meant she didn't have one when confronting Nadine Nolasco. She'd witnessed the interaction between Dr. Fremont and Shane's wife, and if the latter treated a stone-cold killer with such hostility, what would she do to an accusatory stranger?

It was hard for Hanna to believe that Nadine conspired to kill her husband, but she knew the depths of depravity a human mind was capable of.

Including locking someone in a cage no bigger than a dog crate, forcing them to do whatever they wanted.

Focus, Hanna.

She pulled up to the mansion, marveling at how big it truly was. Although Leroy hadn't been able to come up with an accurate estimation of Shane Nolasco's net worth, based on his paltry payout from his last fight, it was tough to imagine him being able to afford a place like this.

It was this thought that ran through her mind as she approached the gate and pressed the buzzer. There were three cars in the long driveway, two Mercedes and a Bentley.

When there was no answer, Hanna considered the possibility that Nadine Nolasco owned a fourth car and that it was this one she'd taken to run errands.

Her finger was nearly on the button again, when the intercom burst with life.

"Hello?"

"Hi, my name is Natalia—" Hanna paused. She had intended on putting on an act, becoming her third Natalia of the day, but decided against it.

Something told her that this wasn't going to work here.

"Who is it?" the hoarse voice demanded. "If you're a reporter or a—"

"My name's Hanna and I was hired by Brock Page to figure out what happened to your husband."

There was a short pause.

"No visitors."

Hanna frowned.

Well, she thought, *if I'm going with the truth, might as well bang it out.*

"Mrs. Nolasco, I know about you and Brock. I know that you were having an affair." This time, the pause was initiated by Hanna, and it was for effect.

"And I also know about you and Dr. Fremont. I think it's in your best interest if we have a little chat."

A second passed, then two. On the third heartbeat, Hanna heard a buzz and the gate swung open.

Chapter 54

SCREECH WASN'T SURE WHY he chose to head to Sport Brain instead of Dr. Fremont's home, but when he saw the BMW in the parking lot, he knew he'd made the correct choice.

"Alright, let's assume she's in there and that she's armed. I have Hanna's gun, but there's no way that I'm going to use it."

The last time I used it, someone ended up dead.

"When we go in there, when we confront her with what we know, your job is to have 9-1-1 on speed dial. If anything looks suspicious, I want you to place the call."

Leroy nodded, but there appeared to be something on his mind.

"What? What is it?"

"What if we go in there and she just denies everything? Then what? We just hold her 'til the cops get here? Do we really have enough to exonerate Brock?"

Screech thought about what they'd uncovered and how this thing might play out in court.

The short answer was that it wouldn't; everything they had was circumstantial.

"I don't know, Leroy. I really don't."

"So, we hope she just grows a conscience and turns herself in? Admits everything? Is that the plan?"

Screech closed his eyes.

"Leroy, can you just be quiet? Thanks." He bit his lip. "None of my plans ever seem to work anyway—thank you, Hanna, for pointing that out—so we're just going to wing it."

Screech opened his eyes and found Leroy staring at him.

"Sounds good to me," he said with a shrug.

They stepped out of the car together and approached Sport Brain side-by-side. It went against his better judgment to put Leroy in a potentially dangerous situation, but it also felt good to have someone with him, someone he could count on, someone he'd fought with before.

He would've preferred Drake in this situation, but Leroy was a more than adequate substitute.

The man had grown up a lot since they'd first met, and looking at him now, with the bruises on his chin, and his head held high, Screech decided that there were very few people he'd prefer to have at his side.

Sure, he teased the boy, and his decision-making processes needed refinement, but he was a valuable asset to SLH.

And Screech was grateful to have him on his team.

When he reached the door, he started to knock, but changed his mind and tried the handle. It opened freely.

Once inside, it took him a few seconds to orient himself. The foyer was empty, but the door at the end of a long hallway was not.

Dr. Fremont was inside, sitting on the floor, pages spread all around her.

Screech looked to Leroy and then quickly strode toward the woman's office.

"Dr. Fremont? My name's Stephen Thompson and I'm a PI. Before you get up, know that I'm armed."

The expression on the woman's face made it clear that she hadn't heard them enter. She instinctively went to stand but stopped when Screech inched up his shirt, revealing his badge and gun.

"I'd prefer if you remained seated while we chat. And don't worry about the mess, me and my friend aren't particular."

Chapter 55

NADINE NOLASCO LOOKED CONSIDERABLY worse than the first time Hanna had seen her. Her botoxed face was still smooth and flat, but her hair was a mess and her eyes were red and raw. She was wearing an old, wrinkled cashmere sweater and a pair of jeans.

The smell suggested that she hadn't bathed or changed in a day or two.

"Where's your daughter? Where's Andrea?" Hanna asked, her first concern being the child.

"She's with her grandma," Nadine said softly.

"Good, that means we can talk." Hanna debated saying something along the lines of, I'm sorry for your loss, but decided against it. First, she wanted to find out if the woman was responsible for her husband's murder before offering condolences. "I want you to know that I'm not the police, but a PI. I don't have any handcuffs or anything like that."

I don't even have a gun.

"Brock really hired you?" Nadine Nolasco asked.

Hanna nodded.

"Yeah, he did. He says he had nothing to do with Shane or Mark's murder."

She watched Nadine's face closely and when she mentioned Shane's name, her brow quivered.

"What do you mean? Brock killed Shane in the ring. The ME said so."

And here come the waterworks, Hanna thought. But to her surprise, the woman, who appeared to be overacting, kept the tears at bay.

"Killed and murder are two different things. But we'll get to that. First I want to know why you didn't tell the cops about your affair."

Nadine averted her eyes.

"I—I couldn't… how would that look? Besides, you think that I'm proud of what I did? Of cheating on him?"

Hanna looked around as Nadine whimpered, noticing that the place was a mess. There were dishes piled high in the sink and empty vodka bottles strewn across the counter. There was also a stack of envelopes on the kitchen table. While Hanna was too far away to read any of the return addresses, stacks of letters were usually one of two things: condolences or bills.

In this case, Hanna suspected that they were both.

"I don't know—proud, not proud, whatever. You still cheated on him and now he's dead."

A little harsh, but to the point.

"Yeah, well, I'm *not* proud," Nadine shot back defensively. "I'm not proud of cheating on Shane or asking him to throw the fight. But none of this was supposed to happen. Him dying? It's—I—I can't believe it."

Hanna waited for this new deluge of emotions to pass.

"You and Dr. Fremont had this all planned out, didn't you? Convince your husband to go down in the first. But then you thought maybe he was going to change his mind, so—"

"No," Nadine interrupted. "No, not the *first*; the *fourth*. Shane was supposed to go down in the fourth. That's what Dr. Fremont had suggested to him over their past five or six sessions. *That* was the plan. Shane found out about my cheating and I thought he was going to divorce me. I—I can't—*we* can't afford that. Look at this place… the bills are piling up and Shane only had one or two fights left. At first, he agreed, even though I could tell it tore him up inside."

Nadine took a deep hitching breath.

"At first, but then…"

"…but then he got cold feet. He went to Mark, Brock's manager, and told him all about it. Fuck, he shouldn't have done that."

And there's the motive for killing Mark, Hanna thought, doing her best to suppress a grin that threatened to creep onto her pretty lips.

"So, what? You owed Nick Petrazzino money that you didn't have now and were in a bind. So, you had to make another bet, make sure that this time Shane couldn't pull out of it."

Nadine shook her head.

"No, no—it was over. Dr. Fremont went to visit Shane in the dressing room before the fight, made one last pitch for him to go down in the fourth, but if he didn't, there was nothing we could do. We had no idea what was going to happen in the first. You gotta believe me."

And despite all the evidence, she's still sticking to her story.

"I want to believe you, Nadine, I do. But Dr. Fremont put money on Shane to go down in the first, not the fourth."

"What? No, the *fourth*—we put money on the fourth. Dr. Fremont called her bookie and put twenty-five grand down, all we had. I was there, I *heard* her. Twenty-five to pay out three-seventy-five. Enough to get pay some of these bills and get a head start if Shane went through with the divorce."

Hanna was taken aback by the seemingly genuine nature of these claims.

"Well," she began, trying not to let her confusion show. "I hate to break it to you, but your friend Dr. Fremont? She told you a lie; Dr. Fremont put a hundred grand on your husband to go down, and stay down, in the first round."

Chapter 56

DR. FREMONT DIDN'T PUT up much resistance at all. Once pressed, she opened up, which was surprising for a cold-blooded killer.

She readily admitted to her gambling debts, her relationship with Nick Petrazzino, and the fact that she'd used information garnered from private sessions to influence her betting patterns.

But, according to her, this was the first time she tried to coach someone into taking a dive, to directly affect the outcome of a live sporting event.

"It was harder than I thought," Dr. Fremont said. "I kept telling Shane to go down in the fourth. You see, I knew about his financial troubles, the fact that his wife spent money like he was Floyd Mayweather and not Shane Nolasco. It was working, too, but then he suddenly just changed his mind. That's when I had to get Nadine involved, to try to push the needle. It still didn't work."

"Wait," Screech interrupted. "The fourth round? Shane was supposed to take a dive in the fourth."

Dr. Fremont, still seated on the floor with her notes spread out all around her, nodded.

"Yeah, the fourth. That's what I—we—put money on."

Leroy and Screech exchanged glances. As Screech pressed for more, his partner reached into his pocket and withdrew the betting sheet he'd obtained from Nick.

"What do you mean, the fourth? You knew that he was going down in the first and not getting up. Mark must've found out about what you'd planned, and that's why you shot him."

Dr. Fremont shook her head vehemently.

"No. That's insane. I tried to rig the fight, but I didn't kill anyone. Jesus. I came here tonight to get my files on both of them and then go to the police and admit what I did—which is try to rig the fight, that's it. But someone broke in and stole all my session notes."

A single word flashed in Screech's mind: *Hanna*. He shook his head disapprovingly.

"But you bet on a first-round knockout."

Dr. Fremont started to get upset now.

"You keep saying that, but it isn't true! I bet on the fourth."

"Dr. Fremont, we know that you put a hundred grand on a first-round knockout and we also know that you visited Isaac Innovations to get some non-New…"

"Non-Newtonian fluid," Leroy finished for him.

Dr. Fremont gripped her forehead.

"Non-what? Isaac… What? I—I—I have no idea what you're talking about. You can call Nick Petrazzino if you want, check my damn bet."

She started to rise, but Screech shook his head.

"I'd feel more comfortable if you remained seated."

Dr. Fremont threw her hands up.

"This is insane!"

Leroy leaned over and showed Screech a sheet of paper. He looked at the numbers for a moment, before offering Leroy a confused expression.

The man placed his finger beneath Dr. Fremont's name and whispered, "She put twenty-five K on fourth."

Screech let this sink in.

She bet on the fourth and *the first? Why would she do that?*

But he realized that the *why* didn't matter, and she could deny having a hand in Shane and Mark's death all she wanted, but that didn't make it any less true.

"Dr. Fremont, there's a man who is going to be convicted of killing his friend, and he's probably going down for Mark Magnusson's murder as well, even though he had nothing to do with that. It's been a long day. Why not just get it off your conscience? You doctored Brock's gloves so that Shane would get knocked out, and when Mark found out what you'd done, you went to his place and killed him."

"This is crazy... I've never been to Mark Magnusson's house. Never even met the man."

"Sure—"

"Dr. Fremont, do you have a Gmail account?" Leroy suddenly asked.

Screech had no idea where he was going with this but let him run with it.

"A what?"

"A Gmail account—one that's synced to your phone."

Dr. Fremont was just as confused as Screech now.

"Yeah," she admitted. "But I made my bets with Nick by phone, not email."

Leroy shook his head.

"You say that you've never been to Mark's house, and now is your chance to prove it."

"How?"

"All I need is a computer and your Gmail account... oh, and your password, of course."

Chapter 57

HANNA DIDN'T NEED A background in psychology to know that Nadine Nolasco was telling her the truth. There were some things that you just couldn't fake and barring a rare split-personality disorder or severe cognitive dissonance, Nadine didn't know how her husband really died.

That didn't mean that what the woman had told her made complete sense, however.

Hanna was getting up to leave, to let Screech in on what she'd learned when Nadine's demeanor suddenly changed.

She went from distraught to desperate in a heartbeat.

"I'll turn myself in," the woman nearly gasped. "I'll turn myself in if it means that Brock stays out of prison. I'll do it. I'll do whatever you want. He didn't know anything — shit, he was probably the only person who didn't know about throwing the fight. I didn't kill my husband, and I didn't kill Mark Magnusson, but if it helps Brock, I'll say whatever you want."

Hanna stared deeply into Nadine's eyes, once again confirming that while the woman was overrun by feelings of guilt, they were the result of infidelity and not murder.

She sighed.

"A little advice?" she said quietly. "If I were you, I'd just keep everything you told me to yourself. *Everything*."

With that, Hanna left the mansion with an overwhelming sense of dread hanging over her.

They'd gotten it all wrong. Screech, Leroy, and she had gotten it wrong from the very start.

Chapter 58

"**GOOGLE TRACKS YOU WHEREVER** you go, so long as you have a Gmail account and your phone on you at the time. Even if location services are off, you can be traced through your email address."

Leroy rolled back the clock on the map in the browser as he spoke. He adjusted it to the night of the fight, and then slowly played it forward. It was like watching one of those old Atari video games, what with a red snake-like line moving around the map. It started at MSG, but around eleven, the line suddenly left the area at a higher rate of speed.

"No," Dr. Fremont muttered.

The line stopped at Mark Magnusson's address just before midnight.

Leroy leaned away from the computer.

"You were there," he said proudly.

Dr. Fremont shook her head.

"I wasn't. I left before the fight even started and went right home."

"Linda, it's right there, on the screen," Screech implored, annoyed that she still insisted on denying it.

"I went right home and watched the fight on TV. I was… I had to find a way to get some money to pay Nick… I spoke to a car… a… a chop shop… he gave me a thousand bucks in advance for my BMW…"

Screech thought back to the recording he'd seen of the crowd at MSG as Dr. Fremont continued to break down.

"You left alright," he said, remembering the empty seat that she'd once occupied. "But not to go home."

"I didn't go there!" she insisted.

"Well, your phone certainly did," Leroy said.

"W—w—wait… I didn't have my phone that night. That's why I had to go home to call the chop shop guy… to use my home phone. I lost my cell the day of the fight. I don't even know where it is now."

Screech tilted his head to one side disapprovingly.

"Convenient," he remarked. It didn't matter now if she confessed or not. This GPS magic that Leroy had conjured was the first concrete evidence they had.

And combined with everything else they knew, he was positive it was enough to get Brock out.

Screech pulled his cell phone from his pocket and dialed Detective Dunbar's number. The man picked up on the first ring.

"Screech, I—"

"We've got her," Screech said, not bothering to hide his enthusiasm now. "We've got her."

"You've got who? Screech, that gun you—"

"Dr. Linda Fremont. She was Shane Nolasco's and Brock Page's psychiatrist. She tried to get Shane to throw the fight, and when he didn't she did something to Brock's gloves. When Mark—"

Dr. Fremont started to protest again, but Screech stepped back into the hallway.

"—when Mark found out, she killed him."

"Yeah, but that gun—"

A flurry of movement caught his eye, and Screech looked up. His first thought was that Dr. Fremont was attacking Leroy, but then he realized that she was back on the floor and the frantic gestures were by design.

Leroy had his own phone pressed to his ear and was making large circles with his free hand.

"What? Who is it?" Screech demanded.

Leroy suddenly went pale.

"It's one of Nick's guys and he... he says that Dr. Fremont just called him, that she wants to arrange a meet-up to collect her winnings."

Chapter 59

LEROY COVERED THE PHONE with his hand.

"What do I do? What do I say?"

Dunbar's voice was still coming through the speaker of his own cell phone, but Screech didn't hear a word the man was saying.

"Screech? Dr. Fremont… uh… wants to… fuck, did you hear me?"

What the hell is going on here? Screech wondered.

"What do I do?"

Leroy was desperate now and Screech looked to Dr. Fremont on the floor.

Was this just a ploy, a deranged alibi of some sort? Or did someone else have Dr. Fremont's phone and was posing as her this whole time?

"Screech!"

"Tell him to keep her there," he said at last.

"What?"

"Tell whoever the fuck is on the phone to meet Dr. Fremont and keep her there. Ask where they're meeting, and we'll go to them."

Leroy, looking very much afraid now, brought the phone back to his ear.

"Uh, Oscar? Yeah, um, this is going to sound a little weird, but can you do me a favor?"

He waited.

"Yeah, can you keep Dr. Fremont with you when you meet her? I really need to talk to her."

Leroy's entire face scrunched.

207 PRIZED FIGHT   207

"Right, yeah, and you're meeting at *Taglia's?* What—oh, yeah, of course not. No, of course. Five minutes that's all I need, yep. Thanks."

Leroy lowered the phone.

"He hung up."

"But did he say where they were going to meet?" Screech asked anxiously.

"Yeah, he said he would hold her for ten minutes, no longer. And I don't think that this Oscar guy fucks around a lot if you know what—"

Screech clapped his hands together.

"All right, let's go, let's go," he exclaimed, gesturing for Leroy to hurry.

"What about her?" Leroy asked, hooking a thumb at Dr. Fremont who was still sitting on the floor looking confused.

Screech didn't know what this second Dr. Fremont thing was all about, but he wasn't convinced that she was innocent. Not yet anyway.

"Dr. Fremont, get your stuff—you're coming with us."

The tired-looking psychiatrist was about to protest, but Screech didn't have time to argue.

"If you really are innocent and want to prove it? If you want to keep Brock Page out of prison, then get your ass in gear and let's get outta here!"

Chapter 60

"I DON'T THINK NADINE knows about the murder, Screech. She admitted to everything else, the infidelity, trying to rig the fight, but not Shane's murder," Hanna said into her phone, shaking her head.

"Hanna, listen," Screech replied frantically. "I need you to meet us at *Barney's*. I have Dr. Fremont in the car with me and Leroy, and we're going to go meet with Oscar, one of Nick's men."

At first, Hanna wasn't sure that she'd heard correctly.

"You have Dr. Fremont in the car with you? And who the fuck is Oscar? Screech, you okay?"

"It's a long story… no time now. Can you meet us there? At Barney's? We have ten minutes, that's it. We need you. Hanna? *Hanna?*"

Hanna didn't answer because both hands were gripping the steering wheel, while her foot jammed the accelerator all the way down.

Chapter 61

"**THAT'S HIM, THAT'S OSCAR** Buglioni," Leroy shouted, pointing a finger at the man with a black ponytail standing outside *Barney's*. He was holding a duffel bag in one hand and there was a black car parked nearby. Screech knew that asking two favors of Nick Petrazzino would come back to haunt them, but they needed to stop whoever was impersonating Dr. Fremont and this was the only way he knew how.

"All right, now we wait and as soon as this person comes, I'm going to confront them. Leroy, you stay here in the car with Dr. Fremont and—"

"Hey, that's Jordyn," Dr. Fremont suddenly said from the backseat. "That's Jordyn, right there."

Screech whipped his head around, wary to take his eyes off Oscar and the money, but there was something in the woman's voice that could not be faked.

"Who?"

Screech's eyes followed Dr. Fremont's now extended finger.

"Jordyn… that's my secretary."

Screech saw a blonde woman with glasses step out of a Mercedes and make her way across the street. From a distance, the similarity with Dr. Fremont was striking. Holding his breath, he continued to watch as this Jordyn made as if to enter *Barney's*. But just when he thought that this was all just a strange coincidence, she made a hard right and started walking directly toward Oscar.

"What is she doing here?" Dr. Fremont asked absently.

"Dr. Fremont, have you ever heard of Isaac Innovations before?" Leroy suddenly asked.

Dr. Fremont shook her head, keeping her eyes on Jordyn the entire time.

"I told you before, I don't—wait, I have heard of them... shit, Jordyn's husband—her *ex*-husband—used to work for them."

"You sure?" Screech demanded.

"Yeah, yeah, pretty sure."

Screech turned to Leroy.

"Give me your phone," he demanded. When Leroy just looked at him, he repeated the instruction, this time more aggressively. "Give me your phone!"

Leroy handed it over and Screech quickly dialed his own number. He answered his phone and then turned on the recording function that he'd installed long ago when he was hoping to catch Bob Bumacher in a trap.

With a deep breath, he held Leroy's phone out to Dr. Fremont. Screech knew he was taking a chance here, a *big* chance, but if he was right about this whole thing, this was an opportunity to not only free Brock but to capture the person who was responsible for two murders.

"Put it in your pocket," he told the frightened looking psychiatrist. "I want you to go out there and speak to your secretary. Get her talking, tell her that you know what she did."

Dr. Fremont shook her head.

"No, I can't, I—"

"You can, and you will. Because if that woman takes the money and leaves here, we'll never see her again. And either you or Brock or Nadine will take the fall for Mark and Shane's murders. That's a promise. Now take the damn phone and get her to talk to you."

Dr. Fremont looked to Leroy for support, but the man was on board.

Eventually, she reached out and took the phone.

Screech looked backed to Oscar and was relieved to see that he was speaking to Jordyn now, clearly stalling.

Two favors, he thought. *We owe one of the most powerful mobsters in the city two favors.*

Screech shook his head.

"Go," he ordered Dr. Fremont. "Go now and whatever you do, keep that woman talking."

Chapter 62

DR. LINDA FREMONT NEARLY stumbled getting out of Screech's car. She felt lightheaded, confused, disoriented. Everything that had happened since the fight was a horrible nightmare.

She wasn't even sure what she was doing now, or why. All she knew was that the scary men in the car would not be happy if she messed this all up.

"Jordyn?" Dr. Fremont called as she made her way across the street.

Her secretary of the last three years didn't seem to hear her; she was preoccupied discussing something with the man with the ponytail.

"Jordyn?" she said a little louder.

This time, the woman's blonde head tilted. Upon the third mention of her name, Jordyn finally turned around. When her eyes met Dr. Fremont's, they visibly widened.

"Linda? What the hell are you doing here?"

"What… what are *you* doing here?"

The glasses that Jordyn was wearing, which Linda had never seen her wear before, slipped down her nose.

The two women stared at each with matching shocked expressions on their faces for a good minute before Jordyn started to smile.

"I'm here to collect my winnings," she said, matter-of-factly. "That's what I'm here to do."

Behind Jordyn, Linda saw Oscar start to slink away, duffel in hand.

"What did you do?" Linda asked, her throat tight. "Jordyn, what did you do?"

They were only four feet apart now, and even though Linda had spent nearly every working day with this woman, she didn't recognize her.

"What did I do? I told you what I did. I placed a bet, and now I'm here to collect." Jordyn turned to Oscar, but the man was already at his car and was climbing into the backseat. "Hey! *Hey!*"

The car door slammed and then it took off.

Jordyn's face was red with fury now.

"You fucked everything up, you know that?" Jordyn pointed a finger at Dr. Fremont's chest as she spoke. Even though she never came close to making contact with Linda, it felt as if that finger was a knife piercing her skin. "This is all your fault."

"What are you talking about?"

"You can't be that stupid, can you? You think I can't hear everything you say to your clients in that room of yours? Huh? And all those bets you made... did you ever think of letting me in on them? Even after my husband got fired from Isaac Innovations—for sleeping with a goddamn co-worker, no less—did you ever once think to try and help me out, so I can pay the bills he left me with?"

Dr. Fremont was speechless.

"I listened to every call you made to your bookie, and I listened to you speak for hours on end in your office. Pretending to be you? Easiest thing in the world."

"I don't... I don't understand."

"Yeah, sure you don't. I knew that Shane was never going to take a dive. Shit, the real mystery is how *you* couldn't tell this from the very start. Some psychologist you are."

"What did you do?" Linda asked again.

"Your lame last-ditch effort to try and get Shane to go down... and then to tell Brock to take him out in the fourth? It was never going to work. But getting MSG to shut off the cameras based on doctor-patient confidentiality? That was a nice touch."

Linda shook her head.

"This is crazy."

"No, not crazy. You were hugging Brock, whispering sweet nothings in his ear... he didn't even see me in the room. Didn't notice a little Liquid Armor injection in his gloves, either."

Dr. Fremont's heart was thumping in her chest.

"Shane died, Jordyn. He *died*."

She shrugged.

"Yeah, he died, so what? He lived a good life. A good, *rich* life."

Linda tried to swallow, but the lump in her throat got stuck.

Screech's words echoed in her head: *Whatever you do, keep her talking.*

"And Mark? Brock's manager?"

"I had no choice. He saw me sneaking into Brock's dressing room after the fight in all the chaos and confusion. Saw me taking his boxing gloves. As I said, I had no choice."

Dr. Fremont took a cautious step backward.

Who are you?

"Why didn't you come to me? If you were this desperate for money, why didn't you come to me?"

Jordyn laughed.

"I *did* come to you. You just never listened because your problems and your patients' problems were always more important."

Dr. Fremont resisted the urge to cast a glance over her shoulder. She hoped that Screech and Leroy were coming out of the car, hopefully with police backup.

"Jordyn, Brock is in jail for something that you did. He—"

"Yeah, that was a nice touch, wasn't it? All it took was a message from Mark and he came running. I knew he'd pick up that gun, implicate himself. It was almost too easy.

"But Brock didn't do anything to you."

"He didn't do anything? Really?" Jordyn suddenly strode forward and reached for Dr. Fremont. She managed to avoid the grasp, but then stopped when she saw the gun.

At some point during this diatribe, Jordyn must have pulled the diminutive pistol from her pocket. And now, instead of a finger, the barrel was pointed at Dr. Fremont's chest.

"Brock slept with a married woman… as far as I'm concerned, he's getting what he deserved, too. As for you… you owe me some money. Lots of money."

Jordyn reached for her again and this time because Linda was distracted by the gun, she pulled back too slowly. The woman's grip was so tight on her upper arm that Linda cried out and tried to break free.

But the gun that was now pressed to her sternum significantly dampened her efforts.

"Please," Dr. Fremont pleaded. "I didn't—"

The other woman came out of nowhere. One minute, Jordyn was squeezing her arm, holding the gun to her chest, the next, she was flat on her back.

Before Dr. Fremont knew what was happening, this third woman kicked the gun away and then pounced on top of a dazed Jordyn, pinning her to the ground.

Natalia Abramovsky slowly turned and looked up at Dr. Fremont, a grin on her face.

"You know what? I think you just fixed my backhand. Thanks, doc."

Chapter 63

SCREECH AND LEROY WERE so enthralled by Jordyn's confession that when things quickly started to turn south, they were too slow to react.

As soon as he saw the gun, Screech immediately jumped out of the car, but he was too far away and too slow to intervene.

Enter Hanna.

Screech was watching in horror, thinking that he had just gotten Dr. Fremont killed, when Hanna sprinted up from behind and delivered one of the most solid punches he'd ever seen to the back of Jordyn's head.

The blonde woman went down like a stone.

By the time Screech crossed the street, Hanna had everything under control, including pinning Jordyn to the sidewalk.

"Hanna, you all right?"

She looked up at him.

"Oh, fancy seeing you guys here. Just in the nick of time, I might add."

Jordyn grumbled something but with a mouth full of blood, her words were impossible to make out.

"I got you on tape," Screech said. "I've got everything—"

The door to *Barney's* opened and two large humans whom Screech recognized as the men Drake affectionately referred to as Tweedledee and Tweedledum came lumbering out.

"Screech?" one of them asked.

Screech acknowledged them, then squinted.

"Hey, you guys think you can do me a favor?"

Dumb looked at Dee, and Dee looked at Dumb.

"Sure."

"Think you can keep her occupied for a few minutes, I've got a call I need to make."

Hanna got off Jordyn, and the feisty woman immediately tried to scramble to her feet and bolt.

But Tweedledee reached down and wrapped his large arms around her. She gave up almost instantly.

"Thanks," Screech said, looking down at his phone. After making sure that the conversation between Dr. Fremont and Jordyn had been recorded, he sent it to Detective Dunbar along with a photo of Jordyn in front of *Barney's.*

"That should do it," he said. "The cops are going—"

His phone buzzed, alerting him of a new message. Only Screech was surprised to see that it wasn't from Dunbar, but a number he didn't recognize.

He opened it and then clicked on the image.

"What?" he gasped.

"Screech? What's going on?" Leroy asked.

Screech looked up at Tweedledee and Tweedledum.

"Think you can hold her for a bit, until the cops get here?" he asked, ignoring his partner's comment.

They both nodded in unison.

"Sure."

"Wait, where are we going?" Hanna demanded.

Screech slowly turned his phone around, showing her the photograph of the USB key that the anonymous number had sent him.

"To finish another job, that's where."

Chapter 64

"**WHAT'S THE PLAN?**" **HANNA** asked as they pulled up outside the address that the mysterious man with the USB had given them.

Before them was a large building with boarded up windows. Screech guessed that it might have once been a restaurant, but he wouldn't have been surprised if someone told him it was a retail outlet, either.

"No plan," Screech said bluntly, looking up and down the street for any signs of life.

"What do you mean, no plan?" Hanna demanded.

Screech shrugged.

"No plan. Every time I come up with a plan, things go wrong. Ask Leroy; I had no plan when it came to Dr. Fremont or her psycho secretary and that seemed to work out. So, yeah, no plan."

Screech was surprised by the resistance; he thought Hanna would've loved this idea.

"We *need* some sort of plan."

Screech shook his head and got out of the car, making sure that Hanna's gun was tucked in his waistband.

"They want either money or something else," he said to Hanna who followed him up to the front door. "We'll just have to give it to them. If it's a fight they want, well, we've got Tyrone and your right hand."

"That's not a plan," Hanna whined as she hurried to catch up to him. Leroy took up the rear.

With his head held high, Screech reached for the door and pulled the handle, half expecting it to be locked.

It wasn't.

Inside, there was a single table in the center of a dusty open space, with a sole light bulb hanging from a cord above it. The poor lighting and covered windows made it nearly impossible to make out much else.

It dawned on Screech that this might not be about the USB at all; it could be just someone from Drake's past wanting to settle the score, take them out one by one.

But this didn't change anything; if they didn't get that USB, it would only be a matter of time before Nick tracked them down and introduced them to heavy-soled shoes and a deep tub.

"Well," he shouted into the darkness, "you asked for me to come here. And now I'm here. Show yourself."

When there was no answer, Screech felt foolish but continued anyway.

"Do you have the USB or not?"

A man emerged from the shadows. He was about six-feet tall, with brown hair and hazel eyes. There was stubble on his cheeks and chin, but it was what he had in his hand that held Screech's attention: a plastic bag with a USB key inside.

"This is the USB you're looking for," the man said calmly. "But it's not yours, it's mine. I want you to tell Nick Petrazzino that we acquired the USB key. I also want you to tell him that he will only be doing business with me from now on."

What the hell? This is all about a PI contract?

"I think you're probably better off just handing it over and forgetting this ever happened," Screech said, mildly disappointed at how anticlimactic this meeting was. "I don't know how you got it, but—"

"It's you," Leroy suddenly said. "It's you—you're the one who told me to pick up my bottle, not to litter."

The man started to grin. And Screech clued into what had happened.

He had been tailing Leroy and Hanna, and when they'd taken the USB key from the DA, he'd stolen it from them.

Hmm, not bad. I'm impressed.

But none of this mattered.

"I'm tired, bored. If you give me the USB key now, I won't tell Nick Petrazzino that you stole it from us."

The man's grin didn't falter, and Screech started to get annoyed.

"All I have to do is make one call, tell Nick what you've done, and you're going to regret ever stepping foot in Central Station."

The man continued to smile—if anything, it grew bigger— which was disconcerting, to say the least.

Clearly, he was aware of who Nick was and yet he seemed unconcerned about the consequences of his actions.

Screech sighed.

"I will—" The man suddenly took another step forward, and his face became fully illuminated for the first time. "Shit."

Screech recognized him, now. He had visited SLH Investigations just as Hanna's painting had arrived, after the disaster at the Loomis Estate.

He'd even given Screech his card: *Hart Investigator*.

"Yeah, I'm guessing you recognize me now," Mackenzie Hart said. "The thing is, I pretty much guessed what you would say, that you would threaten to tell Mr. Petrazzino about this little USB. So, I made sure to cover my ass."

The man gave a shrill whistle and the shadows once again came to life.

Like Mackenzie, this man was also holding a plastic bag. Only there was no USB in this one; instead, there was a gun.

"Jimmy?" Leroy gasped.

Screech's eyes darted first to Leroy, and then to the man holding the gun.

The lighting wasn't great, but he was positive that it was, indeed, Jimmy, Hanna's savage of an ex-husband who had thrown him onto his desk.

"Hanna? What the hell is going on here?" Screech said, feeling his composure start to crumble.

But Hanna didn't answer. When he looked over at her, Screech was confused.

She bowed her head and remained silent.

"Hanna?"

Mackenzie Hart laughed.

"You still don't get it, do you, Screech? How do you think we knew you were going to take DA Trumbo when you did? You think we just followed you around every day for the past month? Got lucky, maybe?"

Screech swallowed hard and stared at Hanna, but she refused to meet his gaze

"This can't be happening," he grumbled.

"Oh, it's happening. Go on, Hanna, tell him. Tell him, or I will."

Hanna, shaking now, said, "I'm sorry, Screech."

Screech felt like he'd been punched in the chest.

"Hanna, please."

He almost reached for her as she made her way across the floor and took up residence beside Mackenzie. Leroy went as far as to take three steps forward before Screech put his arm out and stopped his forward progress.

Leroy reached for her, but Screech held his arm out in front of him, protecting him the way he should have done all this time.

"Looks like you didn't know Hanna as well as you thought you did. And it looks like Hanna wanted to work for a PI firm that could pay her what she's worth. Which is, by my estimation, more than a painting, even one from the Loomis silent auction."

"What do you—" Screech fell silent.

He was suddenly transported back to the moment before he shot Captain Loomis. In the distance, he'd spotted two sets of eyes trained on him.

One had been Hanna's and the other had been this man's.

"What do I… want? Is that what you were going to ask?" Screech nodded feebly.

"I already told you what I want. I want Nick Petrazzino's business. You give me that, and I'll tell Jimmy here to get rid of the gun you used to kill Captain Loomis."

"What is he talking about?" Leroy wheezed.

Somehow, Screech managed to wave a hand and silence him.

The whole ex-husband thing had been a ploy, he realized. A ploy set up by Mackenzie and Hanna to get the gun from his desk.

And it had worked better than any plan Screech had ever come up with.

"And before you ask, yes, it is *that* gun."

Screech glared at Hanna, unable to believe the depths of her betrayal.

"Take your cell phone out and call Nick," Mackenzie ordered, his smile gone now.

Screech saw no way out of this and did as he was asked. But when he pulled out his cell phone, he saw that he had three missed calls, all from the same number: Dunbar's number.

Not only that, but there were a handful of text messages from the man as well.

Pretending to be scrolling for Nick's number, he quickly read the man's messages.

The first message read, *I need to talk to you about the gun.*

The second was the same, as was the third, but the fourth was more telling.

The gun you gave me wasn't used to kill Mark Magnusson.

Screech looked up and stared at the bag that Jimmy, if that was indeed his real name, was holding.

It certainly looked like the gun that he'd used to kill Captain Loomis. And there were no other guns in SLH Investigations.

With a shaking finger, he continued to buy time as he tried to work through everything.

"Any day, Screech," Mackenzie taunted.

If the gun that he'd given Dunbar wasn't the one that killed Mark, then it could only be the one that he'd used to kill Captain Loomis.

But that didn't make any sense. After taking the gun from Brock, he'd put it in the safe where it had stayed until he took it out and brought it to Dunbar himself.

Either Dunbar was mistaken, or somehow the guns had been switched.

"Screech?"

But neither Hanna nor Leroy had the code to the safe.

And Dunbar didn't make mistakes.

Screech suddenly looked up, his eyes blazing, a smile creeping onto his own lips.

There were only two people in the entire world who knew the combination to that safe.

Screech and…

Chapter 65

"DRAKE? OH MY GOD, is that really you?"

Once again it was Leroy calling out names.

Screech's eyes nearly bulged out of his head. He couldn't believe it and had to blink three or four times to make sure that it really was Drake standing behind Jimmy. And even then, he thought that it might just be Drake's brother, Dane, and not Damien. This man before him was thinner and looked healthier than Drake had since… well, since Screech had ever known him.

But when Drake just jammed his hands in his pockets and shrugged, Screech was convinced.

So too was Mackenzie Hart, it seemed.

"Ah, Damien Drake, so nice to finally meet you," he said. "I've heard a lot about you."

Drake smiled.

"I bet you have."

"But it seems like your little vacation has gone to your head… See this woman, Hanna? She's with me now. So, you should be on that side, with Screech and Leroy."

Drake raised an eyebrow but said nothing.

"I was just telling your partners there that if they don't call Nick Petrazzino, I'm taking the gun that Screech used to kill Captain Loomis to 62nd precinct."

"Really?" Drake said, sounding genuinely surprised. "Well, if you're gonna do that, I would make pretty damn sure that you have the right gun."

For a fraction of a second, Mackenzie Hart faltered.

"Oh, I'm sure. My man Jimmy here took it from your little shop and brought it to my place."

"Huh. You mean the building on 41st and 9th? The one on the third floor with the brown door?"

Mackenzie Hart pressed his lips together tightly but didn't say anything.

"The place with 'Hart Investigator' in the window? Cute name, by the way. Let me guess, you have one of those fancy electronic door locks... the kind that has a code... uh... what is it..." Drake snapped his fingers. "Ah, the code... 647231, right?"

McKenzie Hart still said nothing.

"I'm guessing that your desk is the one near the window — you strike me as a window-type of guy. Nice desk, too. Problem is, the lock? Let's be honest, you skimped on it, didn't you?"

Mackenzie turned to stare at Jimmy.

Screech was trying to keep up with what was going on when he saw a strange smile appear on Hanna's face.

"So, let me ask you this, friendo, how confident are you that the gun your henchman is holding is the *right* gun. How confident are you that I didn't sneak into your office and switch it with another gun with a history? Hmm?"

Screech had to give Mackenzie Hart credit. Despite the taunting, he refused to play Drake's game. The problem with that approach was, Screech knew that Drake didn't give a shit if you played his game.

Because everyone already knew who was going to win.

"The real question you should be asking yourself," Drake continued, "is if this isn't the gun that was used to kill Captain Loomis, then what gun did Screech hand over to Detective Dunbar?"

Hanna suddenly took a step away from Mackenzie.

Drake snapped his fingers again.

"Wait, you weren't stupid enough to put your prints all over that gun in the bag, were you? I mean, before you put it in your desk."

Mackenzie grumbled something inaudible.

"Jimmy…"

The big man in the overcoat shrugged. Clearly, he was lost.

"So, if that isn't the gun that killed Captain Loomis, then… ah, I shouldn't be the one to tell you. I'll let a friend do the honors."

Another man stepped from the shadows, surprising everyone but Drake.

"Detective Dunbar?"

The man had a set of handcuffs in his hands and he quickly slapped them on Mackenzie before he even realized what was happening. Then he snatched the bag from Jimmy.

"That would be the gun that killed Mark Magnusson, Drake," Dunbar proclaimed. "And seeing as I am hard of hearing, and I have no idea what you guys were talking about, I can only assume that you, Mackenzie Hart, are an accessory after the fact."

"Indeed," Drake agreed. "You see, the moment you reached out to my friend Hanna here, Mac, she called me. And the one thing I don't do is leave my friends hanging. We came up with a plan, Hanna and I. Earmuffs, Dunbar—after you stole Screech's gun, I stole it back, and switched it."

Dunbar tugged on Mackenzie's wrists, pulling him toward the door.

They'd taken three or four steps before Mackenzie planted his feet.

"You got me, Drake. I'll admit it, you got me."

Drake smiled, and Leroy went to him and gave him a big hug.

"What can I say," Drake began, gesturing for both Hanna and Screech to come over. "I guess I'm just the better—"

"But I got you, too," Mackenzie said with a grin.

Drake stopped smiling.

"I'll admit it, this is not the way I saw this going down, but I knew you'd come back. I knew that someone would reach out to you, somehow, and let you know that Screech was in trouble. I have one more surprise, Drake, and I'm pretty sure you're going to like this one."

Immediately, Screech's mind turned to Jasmine and Drake's baby, to Clay.

There's no way. There's no way this man would—

"Officer Kramer, you can come out now."

"No," Screeched moaned.

But there he was: Officer Kramer, the man who Mandy had brained and the one that Drake had thrown into the shipping container. The one who had put the warrant out for Drake's arrest.

"Damien Drake, put your hands behind your back," Kramer said. When Drake didn't immediately obey, he added, "Don't make me use this gun... on second thought, go right ahead. Because I would like nothing else than to make you hurt."

Epilogue

SCREECH WAS MOVING TOWARD the doors of *Taglia's* when they suddenly opened and a familiar man with a ponytail stepped out.

It was Oscar Bugilioni.

"What do you want?"

Screech took a step back and looked up at the sign. He considered saying, a sandwich or homemade pasta but decided that sarcasm was not the right play here.

"I've got something for your boss," he said instead.

A second man, this one much larger than the first, came out of *Taglia's* and started to pat him down. His meaty fingers found the USB key still in the plastic bag, and he pulled it out.

"I see you came through in the end," Oscar said with a greasy smile. He took the USB key from the security guard.

"Sure did."

"All right, I'll give this to the boss. You can go now."

Screech shook his head.

"I would like to speak to him."

Oscar eyed him with a sneer and eventually indicated the door with his chin.

"Come with me."

Screech hurried after the man, following him through the main dining area, then a hallway, then a back room.

Seated at a large table was Nick Petrazzino.

Oscar walked up to him, whispered something in his ear, and then set the USB drive on the table.

Screech had hoped that the man would smile, or offer something to show that he was pleased, but he didn't. He only gestured for Screech to take a seat, and he quickly obliged.

"Any problems getting the USB key?" Nick asked. As he spoke, his hand slipped below the table and out of sight.

"No, not really," Screech lied.

"And, as per our agreement, you didn't look at what is on the key, correct?"

"Correct."

Nick brought his hand back up and in it were two neat stacks of bills. He placed them beside each other on the table and Screech saw that they were both held together by yellow bands marked with $10,000.

"One pile for the job the other, a bonus."

Screech would've rejected the bonus on principle if he'd thought the man wouldn't be insulted to the point of violence.

He grabbed the stacks of money.

"You can go now," Nick instructed. "I'll be in touch."

Oscar was suddenly behind Screech, just in case he required further encouragement.

"There's just one more thing."

Nick smirked.

"I figured as much. Let me guess, this has something to do with our mutual friend, Leroy Walker?"

"You guessed right. I was hoping… I was hoping that we could make his favor go away."

Nick stopped smiling.

"And why would I do that?"

Screech leaned to one side and looked down at the black bag resting by Nick's feet.

"Well, because I saved you a whole lot of money, for one; the woman posing as Dr. Fremont is now behind bars. I'm thinking she won't be around to collect her winnings for, oh, thirty years?"

Nick nodded in agreement.

"You're right, but there's something wrong with your math."

Screech frowned.

"Excuse me?"

"Well, I'd say me helping Leroy with the betting sheets and you guys saving me money is a wash."

"Yeah, that's—"

"—but," Nick continued, raising a meaty finger. "But Leroy asked Oscar here for another favor."

Screech slouched in his chair.

"Yes, keeping Jordyn busy while you came to the rescue. That was another favor, unless I'm mistaken?"

Screech sighed. This was, unfortunately, the way he'd expected things to go.

"Well, then I have another proposal for you. Leroy's just a kid—I'll trade his favor for one of my own."

Nick thought about this for a moment.

"I'll consider it. But there's something you should consider, too."

Screech encouraged the man with a nod.

"When a person owes me a favor, I'm guaranteed to collect. Maybe not in a week, a month, or a year. But I never forget. And if the time comes for me to collect, and you cannot provide me with what I need, I will seek it from someone else. Someone who means something to you, who is important to you. Do you understand what I'm saying, Stephen Thompson?"

Screech swallowed hard.

"I do."

"Then do you want to reconsider exchanging Leroy's favor for one of your own?"

Screech's reply was immediate.

"I don't."

Nick clasped his hands together and leaned forward.

"Okay, then, Stephen Thompson, I accept your proposal. And now, you may leave."

"Thank you," Screech said as he rose to his feet.

As Oscar led him back through the restaurant, Screech thought about what Nick had said.

Not about the favors, but about the USB key.

The man had asked him if he'd looked at what was on it, and when Screech had said he hadn't, he was telling the truth.

But what he'd done was even better.

Screech had made a copy of that USB key.

Because when Nick Petrazzino came calling for his favor, Screech now had something he could use as leverage.

This plan, it seemed, had worked out perfectly.

The End

Author's Note

IT'S BEEN A FEW months since I last left Drake on an island—literally—and I've missed him. I've missed Screech and Hanna and Leroy, too (in case you hadn't noticed).

Drake is and always will be one of my favorite characters. He and his friends are fan favorites, but sometimes that's not enough.

If you want Drake's adventures to continue, there are several ways you can support him. Obviously, the number one thing is to buy this book and read it—which, clearly, you already have. Some other things you can do include writing a review on Amazon for *Prized Fight* and the earlier books in this series. This really helps Amazon promote it to new fans. Speaking of new fans... yep, that's probably the best ways to ensure that Drake keeps on trucking: tell a friend about him, tweet about him, post something on Facebook.

In all seriousness, these things help me figure what book to write next, and which ones you guys will enjoy most.

As always, I'm forever grateful that you've spent you time and money reading one of my books. You guys really are the best fans.

You keep reading, and I'll keep writing.
Pat
Montreal, 2019.

Printed in Great Britain
by Amazon